A DISCOVERY

The dog took a bypath heading toward the Forest of Bondy. Soon they entered the shadow of the green canopy.

As they rode beneath the boughs of the trees, DeNarsac remarked quietly, "This does not bode well," and Thierry noticed that he placed a hand lightly upon his sword. Dragon pressed deeper and deeper into the trees, until they came to a huge and ancient oak, its roots gnarled and thick, its spreading limbs almost touching the ground.

Dragon halted, then approached a low mound of earth and dead leaves. Whimpering, he lay down on top of it, his head on his paws.

DeNarsac reined his horse and dismounted. Signaling for Thierry to stay where he was, he walked to the dog and knelt beside him. The boy saw that he was choked with emotion, and he knew intuitively what DeNarsac was about to say.

"I fear that Dragon has led us to his master. It is my guess that Montdidier is buried here."

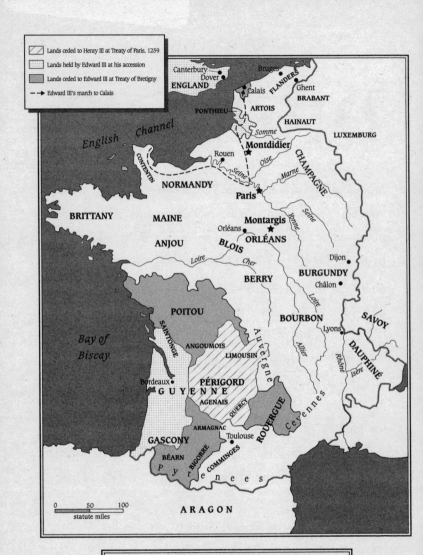

Lands ceded to Henry III at Treaty of Paris, 1259
Lands held by Edward III at his accession
Lands ceded to Edward III at Treaty of Bretigny
Edward III's march to Calais

English Channel

Canterbury
Dover
ENGLAND

Bruges
Calais
FLANDERS
Ghent
BRABANT

PONTHIEU
ARTOIS

HAINAUT

LUXEMBURG

CONTENTIN

Somme

Rouen

Montdidier

Oise
Seine
Marne
CHAMPAGNE

NORMANDY

Paris

BRITTANY

MAINE

ANJOU

Orléans
BLOIS

Montargis
ORLÉANS
Seine
Yonne

Dijon

BURGUNDY

Loire
Cher

BERRY

Châlon

POITOU

ANGOUMOIS
LIMOUSIN
Auvergne

BOURBON

Lyons
SAVOY

Loire
Allier

Bay of Biscay

SAINTONGE

Bordeaux
GUYENNE

PÉRIGORD
AGENAIS
QUERCY
ROUERGUE

Cévennes

Rhône
Isère
DAUPHINÉ

GASCONY

ARMAGNAC
Toulouse

BÉARN
BIGORRE
COMMINGES

P y r e n e e s

ARAGON

0   50   100
statute miles

FRANCE AT THE PEACE OF BRETIGNY
❧✦❧ 1360 ❧✦❧

DRAGON
Hound of Honor

Julie Andrews Edwards
and Emma Walton Hamilton

ADAPTED FROM THE LEGEND OF
THE DOG OF MONTARGIS

THE JULIE ANDREWS COLLECTION
HarperTrophy®
An Imprint of HarperCollinsPublishers

Harper Trophy® is a registered trademark of
HarperCollins Publishers Inc.

Dragon
Copyright © 2004 by Wellspring, LLC
For information address HarperCollins Children's Books,
a division of HarperCollins Publishers,
10 East 53rd Street, New York, NY 10022.

Library of Congress Cataloging-in-Publication Data
Edwards, Julie.
Dragon : hound of honor / Julie Andrews Edwards and Emma
Walton Hamilton.— 1st ed.
    p. cm. — (Julie Andrews collection)
"Adapted from the legend of the dog of Montargis."
Summary: In medieval France, a wolfhound helps solve the
murder of his master, the beloved son of the Count de
Montdidier and leader of the Royal Bodyguard in the court
of Charles V.
    ISBN 0-06-057119-5 — ISBN 0-06-057120-9 (lib. bdg.)
    ISBN 0-06-057121-7 (pbk.)
[1. Knights and knighthood—Fiction. 2. Irish wolfhound—
Fiction. 3. Dogs—Fiction. 4. Murder—Fiction. 5. Middle
Ages—Fiction. 6. France—History—Charles V, 1364–1380—
Fiction.] I. Hamilton, Emma Walton. II. Title. III. Series.
PZ7.E2562Dr 2004   2003025019
[Fic]—dc22   CIP
                                                          AC

Typography by Larissa Lawrynenko
11 12 13 14   LP/CW   10 9 8 7 6 5 4 3
❖
First HarperTrophy Edition, 2005
Visit us on the World Wide Web!
www.harperchildrens.com

For Blake and for Steve—
For their patience, faith, and encouragement

—J.A.E. &
E.W.H.

CONTENTS

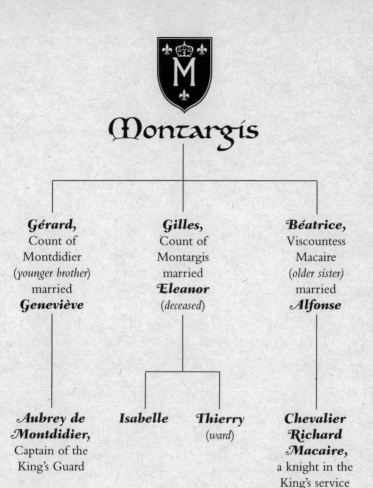

Montargis

Gérard,
Count of
Montdidier
(*younger brother*)
married
Geneviève

Gilles,
Count of
Montargis
married
Eleanor
(*deceased*)

Béatrice,
Viscountess
Macaire
(*older sister*)
married
Alfonse

**Aubrey de
Montdidier,**
Captain of the
King's Guard

Isabelle

Thierry
(*ward*)

**Chevalier
Richard
Macaire,**
a knight in the
King's service

**Guy, Sieur DeNarsac,
Captain of the Count's Men-at-Arms**
A friend who has known
the three families since childhood.

Chapter One

THE REUNION

T HE MORNING WAS FILLED with promise. It was in the quality of light, spreading across the unspoiled countryside—limning every blade of grass, every bush, twig, tree; nature in full glory on a summer day. It was in the air—a gift in itself, dew-freshened, and perfumed with hints of clover and sweetbriar rose carried on a gentle breeze. It would be warm later.

A lark rose from the underbrush, spiraling upward in ever-ascending circles, trilling its hymn of praise. Reaching the peak of its climb, it hung fluttering above the plain as if arrested with wonder at its existence and the beauty of the world beneath.

The dog crested the hill and he, too, paused—front paw raised, alert to every detail, his nostrils sensing rabbit that had passed moments before and the doe and her

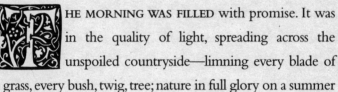

fawn hiding in the forest nearby. He was magnificent, his color white—rare for a wolfhound—and he had a fine head and well-set eyes. He wore no collar, no trimming of any kind, the only tether holding him in check being an innate intelligence and the respect and love he bore his master. Looking back to make sure that he was close, the dog ran on, rejoicing in his exquisite freedom.

Thierry urged his pony in front of the others, eager to be the first to glimpse the horizon. He smiled as he watched the dog cavorting, snuffling, making furrows in the moist green grass. Shading his eyes against the sun, he called, "I don't see anyone yet!"

Two men, riding easily, lazily, came abreast of him and reined in their horses. All three looked down across the plain in companionable silence, broken only by the occasional jingle of harness, the stomp of a hoof, the crunch of a bit.

After a moment, the fair-haired knight spoke. "He said he'd arrive by first light. I've seldom known him to be late."

"He's been traveling over two days," said the other man.

"But he'll be anxious to get here. He wouldn't miss the tourney. It has always been his favorite holiday."

Thierry asked, "Won't he be weary?"

"Macaire?" The fair knight laughed. "Five hours' rest and he'll be like new. I wager he'll be successful tomorrow. Or perhaps our friend DeNarsac here." He indicated their companion.

"I can't wait to compete," Thierry enthused.

"And so you shall, when you are old enough, strong enough, foolish enough," DeNarsac replied gently.

"I've been practicing. I want to be just like you."

"Then you will be broken many times, and you will hurt a great deal. It would sadden me to see that young frame jarred, to see those freckles bloodied." DeNarsac knuckled the boy's dark hair affectionately. "But you show considerable promise for your thirteen years. And I know you are brave."

"And there is the thrill of it, the sport, the triumph," countered the fair knight. "You have always loved it, Guy. Admit it."

Guy DeNarsac shrugged. "I do admit it, but if tomorrow fortune chooses to smile on me, then I shall make it my last tournament. I hope I am sensible enough to know when it is time to stop . . . if I am to have a life after." He rubbed his knee ruefully. "But truly it is you,

Aubrey, who stands to win, even more than Macaire. He has strength, to be sure, but you have quick wits and greater skill."

Aubrey de Montdidier watched as the wolfhound loped away again, then said thoughtfully, "Let us hope tomorrow is the best solstice ever . . . a day to remember. Ho! Dragon!" he called as the dog veered sharply toward the forest. "Not in there. You know better."

Hardly breaking stride, Dragon obediently altered course and circled back to the party, his long legs moving rhythmically, easily.

"He is magnificent, Aubrey," commented DeNarsac. "There is not another like him. He is as intelligent as he is well-bred."

"Indeed. He can anticipate the quick turn of a sword as well as any of us."

"Because you trained him. It is not every knight who improves his sparring through playful practice with his dog. When you breed him, would you consider letting me take a pup?"

Montdidier nodded. "I've been searching for a suitable mate for Dragon. When I find one, it will be my pleasure."

"May he be as fortunate as you with Lady Isabelle," DeNarsac said warmly.

"Look!" Thierry interrupted. "What is that?" In the distance, something bright was moving, gleaming, caught by the sun. "That's Macaire, isn't it? That's his entourage!"

"So it is." Aubrey de Montdidier gathered his slack reins. "What did I tell you? Come, let us see who can be the first to reach my cousin."

The two men and the boy cantered across the plain, with Dragon easily matching their every stride.

The Chevalier Richard Macaire rode out ahead of his men to greet them.

"Aubrey! Guy! How splendid. And Thierry! By my faith, boy, you must have added three inches since I last saw you."

The friends embraced, the horses mingling, jostling one another. Macaire maneuvered his palfrey and they trotted back to join the other riders in his entourage—a valet, two guards, a squire, and a servant leading pack-horses weighed down with equipment.

Macaire announced, "Gentlemen—may I present my cousin Aubrey de Montdidier of the King's Bodyguard, and our friend Guy DeNarsac, Captain of the Count's

Men-at-Arms. This good-looking lad is Thierry, ward of the Count of Montargis. Thierry, you've met Lieutenant Landry, haven't you?" Macaire indicated the earnest young man leading his group.

"I don't believe so, sir." Thierry acknowledged the Lieutenant with a dip of his head.

"Landry was appointed to me when His Majesty gave me my commission," said Macaire.

"How has it been in the field?" Montdidier asked.

Macaire shrugged. "Damp. Dull. Hard work. I'd much prefer to be with you, serving His Majesty in Paris, than in a garrison beating back the English. But my men are good and will be even better when I have finished with them. How goes it with you in that fair city, being so close to King Charles the Wise? It must be intoxicating, all the glory and splendor!"

"It is challenging work, but a great honor nonetheless," Montdidier replied quietly. He glanced approvingly toward a magnificent and powerful horse—a destrier—that Macaire's squire was attempting to calm.

Macaire said gleefully, "I found him a month ago and took him on the instant. He's *superbe*, eh? Wait till you see him in action. You won't have a chance tomorrow, cousin!"

"We'll see, we'll see," Montdidier replied good-naturedly. "But I have a second mount available for you in the event you have need of it."

"We have a splendid tournament planned," said DeNarsac. "Constable Du Guesclin is *en route* to Paris and will be our guest of honor."

Thierry said, "The Count feels this will be the biggest holiday Montargis has ever had. People have come from as far as Amiens and Dijon, and the village is overrun with visitors. Some are even camping near the river or beside the walls of the château."

"I came in from Paris last week and was amazed at how many were here," added Montdidier. "My parents arrived two days ago and couldn't believe the crowds."

"And my mother?" Macaire asked.

"She is here. Longing to see you, of course. Thierry has already felt the lash of her tongue."

"Poor Thierry! How many participants do we have in all?"

"There will be four pairs tomorrow," DeNarsac answered. "You have been matched against Josselin DuBois."

"My old nemesis. Splendid! And the number of courses?"

"Three runs for each challenger."

"The opening banquet is this evening," Thierry added excitedly. "Lady Isabelle has made all the arrangements and has chosen an avian theme this year. All the prizes relate to birds—a peacock, a falcon. The Count has commissioned a magnificent sword with a design of ospreys on the hilt."

"That is generous indeed." Macaire was impressed. "I shall affix ostrich plumes to my helm to be *à la mode*." He grinned and stretched in his saddle. "Ah! It is good to be back. I long for a bath, some refreshment. Would that time could stand still a moment—that it might be like the old days."

"It will be as always," Montdidier reassured him. "Families, friendship. Nothing has changed so much."

"Except for one thing," Thierry reminded him.

"What?" Macaire looked expectantly at the boy, then at Montdidier. "What?"

"*Dites-lui!* Tell him!" Thierry urged.

Montdidier said, "Lady Isabelle has accepted my proposal of marriage."

Macaire was speechless for a moment.

"When?" he finally asked.

8

"Yesterday. The Count gave us his blessing."

"Ahh! You rogue!" Macaire pounded his shoulder playfully. "I am absent three months, and you steal her away."

Ducking the blows, Montdidier laughed. "Steal her? You never had a chance."

"Not true. Not true," Thierry crowed, hugely enjoying the banter.

"Not true indeed." Macaire threw back his head and cried dramatically, "Isabelle! What folly is this?" He glanced sideways at DeNarsac. "A good pairing, wouldn't you say, Guy? The Montargis and Montdidier estates merged. Quite a *coup*." Turning back to Montdidier, he said, "You are to be congratulated, cousin. It is a fine match."

"It is a love match," Montdidier replied quietly. "I adore her—I always have—since we were infants."

"As did we all," acknowledged Macaire. "Do you remember the day we took the horses and raced to the river? She rode bareback, and even then she trounced us. I have loved her ever since. You, too, Guy. I have seen it. You would lose your tongue when she was within a King's foot of you."

DeNarsac nodded, blushing. "*C'est vrai*. But I was simply the Marshal's son, living over the stables. She would never have considered this lumbering frame—not with you two *élégants* around."

"Well, you are right! She must have been hard put to choose between us." Macaire chuckled. "But you, Montdidier! Had I been home but a few days earlier . . . What say, Thierry? How do you feel about your Lady marrying this *brigand*?"

"I am happy," the boy said gravely. "I know she is happy."

"But this is excellent!" Macaire slapped his thigh. "What a tourney this will be. What sport! I will avenge myself by unseating you, cousin. Then I will embrace you and forgive you."

"I wager you will miss me by yards," Montdidier countered.

The party rode on, exchanging pleasantries. Dragon gamboled around them, content in their company, but suddenly he stiffened, looking toward the forest.

Montdidier cautioned, "Dragon. Hold."

"He senses game," observed Macaire knowingly.

"But it is dangerous. Especially this week. I find myself more cautious than usual when I bring him here for morning exercise."

"With the increased crowds, we get more vandals and robbers," DeNarsac explained. "They come for their own sport, I'm afraid. The forest is not safe anymore."

Thierry glanced at the ancient trunks and choking foliage, and a chill pricked his skin as he wondered what evil lay hidden there.

A young doe sprang out from the trees and stood quivering, tense. At sight of the group, she darted left, then broke to the right. Dragon took off after her, reason overwhelmed by the thrill of the chase and the lust in his heart.

"DRAGON!" Thierry called.

Montdidier said, "Let him run. He will not go far."

The men watched as dog and doe tried to outwit each other, cutting diagonals across the plain. The deer leaped for the safety of a thicket and was gone. Panting, frustrated, Dragon resignedly trotted back to the party.

The great château loomed ahead, flags fluttering from every turret. Skirting the village and avoiding the colony of visitors' tents near the river, the men passed the meadow where the tournament would be held on the morrow. They paused, admiring the emerald-green turf, the lists and palisades, and the colorful pavilions already adorned with the formal standards and shields of the challengers. Even at this early hour, groundsmen and carpenters were adding the finishing touches to ensure that all was in readiness for the spectacle to come.

"It is a pretty sight, is it not?" observed Montdidier. "Mark it well, my friends. The grace of this morning is perhaps the last we shall have before the mayhem is upon us."

The party rode across the river bridge and headed for the towering gates of the château. As they clattered under the stone arch, a young woman came running toward them. Scarcely eighteen years of age, she was a grave-faced beauty with white and flawless skin, and Thierry's heart skipped a beat, as it often did at sight of her. Macaire gave a cry of pleasure and, dismounting quickly, swept her into his arms.

"Isabelle! *Chère* Isabelle, you look *ravissante*!"

"Richard. Welcome! How wonderful to see you! I have been looking forward to this moment—to having us all together again."

Macaire held her at arm's length. "So, you could not wait for me? Woman, you have broken my heart!"

She laughed. "Forgive me! Who knew that our cousin who once teased me so mercilessly would grow up to be so irresistible?" She moved to take Montdidier's arm and gently rested her head against his shoulder. "But we will bear charming children, don't you agree?"

"I thought I was the irresistible one?" Macaire joked, his eyes flashing wickedly.

"So you are!" Montdidier bantered. "Every wench in the country will attest to that. But *this* beauty is mine!" He kissed Isabelle lightly on the forehead. "Abandon the pursuit, Richard, and give us your blessing—or we won't ask you to be the ring bearer at the nuptials in July."

DeNarsac winked at Thierry as they dismounted and handed their reins to his squire, Gilbert. They watched the three cousins walk arm in arm across the courtyard.

"'Twas ever thus." DeNarsac grinned. "They are inseparable."

Thierry nodded happily. "For as long as I can remember."

Isabelle called over her shoulder, "Thierry, Guy! Come along, you laggards! You'll miss breakfast!"

13

Macaire groaned with pleasure.

"Ahh! A proper meal! *Quel plaisir!* But first to find my dear mother, before she berates me for not giving her the attention she believes she so richly deserves!"

Chapter Two
THE TOURNAMENT

Y MIDMORNING OF THE following day, the tournament field was swarming with people and the excitement was palpable.

Vendors were doing a brisk trade, selling gourds of pungent ale and weak wine. There was an abundance of meat pies, dried fish, pastries, and sweetmeats. Peddlers offered trays of cheap trinkets. Minstrels played festive music, and jesters accompanied them with bells and cymbals. Entertainers performed in small gatherings: jugglers, dancers, archers demonstrating their talents, actors staging mock sword fights.

Merchants and burghers, ecclesiastics and lesser gentry gathered in a cordoned area immediately below the grand pavilions. The women were dressed in their finest and most colorful attire, and it was their sport to see and be seen.

As the church bells rang the noon hour, Thierry raced from the château and pushed through the crowds toward the lists. Climbing onto a wooden barrier, he scanned the field for DeNarsac and saw him with Gilbert outside a changing tent. Thierry ran to greet them.

"Bonjour!" he said breathlessly. "Lady Isabelle says she has no more need of me today, that I may observe the holiday like everyone else. I'd rather be down here with you and Gilbert than in the pavilion—if that's acceptable," he added hastily.

DeNarsac was checking the painted head defense and chin strap of his gray destrier.

"You may stay," he said quietly. "Hold these." Handing Thierry the horse's reins, he moved to test the girth of the saddle. He was wearing a padded felt tunic and a neck defense of mail. His legs and feet were covered with mail also. Gilbert was laying out the bulk of his master's armor on a bench nearby. He playfully put the padded arming cap atop his ginger hair and struck a pose. Thierry grinned at the young squire and held his thumbs up in mock approval.

He glanced across the barriers and saw Macaire arriving with his entourage and the magnificent, but mettlesome, black destrier. It took the combined strength of Lieutenant Landry and a squire to contain the spirited creature.

DeNarsac's gray pricked its ears and tossed its head. Thierry steadied it and patted its neck.

"Are you ever fearful?" the boy suddenly asked.

DeNarsac looked up, then continued to inspect his tack.

"Yes," he answered. "But that is a good thing. Fear makes one more careful, better prepared."

"Were you serious yesterday when you said this would be your last tourney?"

"Perhaps."

"But I had hopes that I might one day also be your squire."

Gilbert called out, "And how could you be squire to a knight who doesn't fight, or joust, or want to participate?"

DeNarsac smiled at them both and smoothed the green-and-white caparison draped over the gray's quarters.

"I didn't say I wouldn't participate—and there are

times a man *must* fight." He called to Macaire, "Ho, Richard! How fares it with you?"

Macaire had been talking heatedly with Lieutenant Landry, but he answered cheerfully enough.

"Marry, but I'm travel sore! I had a fitful night and I could not wake this morning."

DeNarsac chuckled. "What happened to the Macaire of old, who used to carouse three nights in succession and outlast us all? Perhaps you're not up to the challenge these days?"

"Ha! Your wish, no doubt. I could ride ten courses to your one and still raise a lance." Macaire quaffed a beaker of wine. "But this helps." He grinned.

"Have you seen Montdidier?"

"I have not seen anyone other than my own party. I have been running late all morning."

"Aubrey is late also," observed DeNarsac, scanning the enclosures. "Thierry, have you seen him?"

"No, sir. Not since last night. My lady favored him with a blue kerchief and said she would see him after the tourney. Do you wish me to go and look for him?"

DeNarsac hesitated.

"It is unusual that he is not here. No. You stay with

me. Gilbert can go." He turned to his squire. "Run to the château and inquire of Montdidier's valet. Also ask at the stables. There may be a problem with the horses. Thierry, come help me with my armor."

There was a fanfare of trumpets, and the throng of spectators looked toward the South Gate. A roar of approval erupted as the Count of Montargis and his party rode slowly onto the field, followed by applause, cheers, and shouts as the crowd recognized the Count's guest of honor, Bertrand Du Guesclin. The Constable of France was revered by all—and the crowd's approbation did not diminish as the two men made a dignified tour of the lists. Thierry stood on his toes to catch a glimpse of them.

Du Guesclin was dressed conservatively in plain, black, serviceable clothes. His countenance was pale and pug nosed, but he carried himself with a thoughtful and dignified air.

"He is smaller than I imagined," Thierry confided to DeNarsac.

"Yet he has jousted to great glory," DeNarsac replied. "As a strategist and in matters of diplomacy, he has no equal. He sets a new standard for knighthood."

Riding beside his guest of honor, the Count of Montargis was resplendent in red and black, his voluminous cape caught at the shoulders, spreading behind him across his horse. Looking toward the grand pavilion, Thierry saw the Lady Isabelle sitting sidesaddle on her pretty jennet, an attendant holding the lead rein. Her flaxen hair was coiffed in braids placed either side of her head, and her veil was held by a single gold circlet. She wore a gown of soft blue, the color of cornflowers, with gold trim at the neck and on the hem.

Thierry caught her eye and waved. She lifted an arm in response, her velvet tippet falling back against her elbow. Thierry felt giddy with delight at having received her attention for that brief moment.

Behind Isabelle, servants and grooms escorted a richly decorated wagon pulled by four horses. It carried the remainder of the Count's party: Richard Macaire's mother, the Viscountess Béatrice; Aubrey's mother, Geneviève, Countess of Montdidier; their ladies-in-waiting; and a priest and his deacon. Aubrey's father, Gérard, Count of Montdidier, accompanied them, riding on a handsome palfrey.

Béatrice immediately demanded to be helped from

the wagon and proceeded to the steps of the grand pavilion. A formidable woman, impeccably dressed, she had a permanent expression of dissatisfaction upon her countenance.

Leaning heavily on the arm of her brother, Gérard, she complained, "If my indulgent spouse would curb his excesses and consider someone other than himself, I might burden him rather than you."

"How is your dear Alfonse? We haven't seen him in a while," the Count inquired.

"He is sodden with wine, overweight, and out of sorts," she replied sharply. "Other than that, he is his usual adorable self."

The Count changed the subject. "You have not said how long you intend to stay, sister."

"I shall return as soon as possible. My rooms here are damp, and there is a constant draft. I miss the comforts of home."

Isabelle said, "But Aunt, you must show me what we can do to make you more comfortable."

"I wouldn't know where to begin," Béatrice replied. "The château has barely changed since my childhood. One would think your father would have made more improvements over the years, but I suppose a widower cannot be expected to notice these things." She turned her attention to Du Guesclin, who had just entered the pavilion with the Count of Montargis. "*Monsieur le Connétable!* It is such an *honor* to have you with us! You must sit next to me."

Du Guesclin bowed politely.

"You look fetching, Béatrice," the Count of Montargis boomed as he handed her and the Constable of France goblets of wine.

"An old woman dresses for her son these days," she said. "You have not met my son, the Chevalier Macaire, have you, *Connétable*?"

"It has not been my pleasure, Madame."

"Well, you'll see him soon enough. He will not be bettered this day. You know His Majesty recently assigned him a garrison? I'm heartbroken, of course, that he didn't remain in Paris, but what can one do?"

Isabelle drifted to the front of the pavilion and glanced in the direction of the North Gate, hoping for a glimpse of her betrothed. Looking after her, Du Guesclin remarked to his host, "She has become a great beauty, my friend."

"She is a joy. Would that my beloved Eleanor were

here to see her. They are so very alike."

"You never chose to remarry?"

"I considered it once, but now I am too set in my ways. Isabelle is the lady of the house, and I have all that I need. There is also Thierry, of course."

"Ah, yes, your ward. Refresh my memory regarding his circumstances?"

"His parents were my closest friends. They were brutally assassinated by that peasant uprising—*le Jacquerie*—when he was an infant. The boy would not have survived had not a trusted valet escaped with him and brought him here," the Count explained.

"That is tragic. He is fortunate indeed to have you." Du Guesclin sipped his wine.

"He has become the son I never had. He acquired an inheritance, which I oversee for him until he comes of age. Meanwhile, he is page to Isabelle and she is responsible for his education. In truth, they are like brother and sister." The Count glanced around. "Isabelle, where *is* Thierry?"

"Need you ask, Father? He is with DeNarsac. I sensed he was eager to be with the action, so I gave him his freedom."

* * *

The contenders for the joust were gathering at the North Gate, each accompanied by a squire bearing a spear.

Thierry positioned DeNarsac's gray just behind Macaire's destrier. He felt the excitement within him building. The commotion of horses, their smell, the tense concentration of men bent on a single purpose, the ring and clatter of armor, the din of the crowd, the waving of pennants and scarves—all served to inflame his young passion and quicken his pulse.

"And *still* Aubrey is not here," DeNarsac called to Macaire.

"It is troubling," Macaire acknowledged. "What should we do?"

"We should alert someone, at least," said DeNarsac, and rode forward to confer with the Marshal at the head of the column.

The trumpets sounded, the drums beat a tattoo, and the heralds announced the parade of contestants. Spectators pressed forward, some climbing trees or standing on barriers for a better view.

The Marshal and Assistant Marshal rode onto the field and placed themselves at opposite ends of the lists. Amid the clamor and applause, the knights entered in single file, keeping their magnificent chargers on a tight rein, showing their form and displaying their paces with great horsemanship.

Arriving in front of the grand pavilion, the knights removed their plumed and decorated helms and formed a line. The squires dipped their lances as one, in deference to the nobility before them.

The Count of Montargis stepped forward, and the shouts and acclamations subsided.

"Good citizens, friends, noble knights! I bid you welcome," he called. "I am gratified so many of you have returned to be with us once again and that so many more have been added to that number. Word of our celebrations has spread, and we have become the tournament best known for its sport, the charm of its setting, the goodwill of all who meet here. Nor will you be disappointed this year."

His words elicited enthusiastic applause.

"We are honored to have with us today a special guest

who is eager to see for himself all that Montargis has to offer: Our Constable of France—Bertrand Du Guesclin!"

The throng erupted once more. Du Guesclin acknowledged the ovation, and it was several moments before the Count was able to continue.

"Many of you know our Lady of the Tournament. Arrangements have been in her capable hands, and she will be presenting the winners with their bounty later today. My daughter, Isabelle, *Dame de Montargis*."

From the roar of approval, it was obvious that Isabelle was beloved. Thierry noticed a look of concern upon her brow, but she waved to the crowd and acknowledged all the knights graciously, reserving a warm smile for DeNarsac and Macaire. The latter placed a hand upon his heart in mock despair: a suitor spurned.

Isabelle bowed her head, accepting the compliment; then she turned and said something to her father. He nodded and held up his hand for silence.

"It seems we have only seven of the eight registered contestants. Can the Marshal explain this?"

The Marshal rode to the center of the lists and spoke. "My Lord, the knight Aubrey de Montdidier is not present. Might I suggest that if he does not arrive momentarily, we select a substitute."

The Count glanced toward Isabelle and Aubrey's parents, then said, "Very well. Who will ride in his place?"

Du Guesclin murmured, "Would that I had suitable attire with me, I should volunteer in an instant."

DeNarsac urged his mount forward a pace.

"My Lord, I will happily represent the Honorable Aubrey de Montdidier."

"As will I, my Lord." Macaire moved to his side.

The Count nodded. "So be it. Sieur DeNarsac will ride for Montdidier, if necessary. The Chevalier Macaire will be the second substitute. Let the tournament begin."

Another fanfare, and a herald announced the rules of engagement.

As the riders prepared to exit the field, Béatrice pushed forward.

"Wait!" she cried. Removing her veil, she threw it from the pavilion to her son below. Macaire's squire retrieved it and presented it to him. Macaire kissed it gallantly, but as he turned away, he winked at DeNarsac, then raised his eyes heavenward.

* * *

DeNarsac and his opponent were listed to joust first. Thierry escorted the knight on his gray to the North Gate, and DeNarsac wheeled his horse to face the challenger on the opposite side of the lists. Suddenly, Gilbert pushed through the crowd and ran up to him.

"Milord, it seems Aubrey de Montdidier went riding as usual early this morning. He took the dog with him, but neither has returned. His valet has gone to search for him. His groom wishes to know what he should do, as his destrier is ready for the joust."

Thierry felt a sense of foreboding.

DeNarsac answered swiftly. "Tell the groom to bring the horse. If Aubrey returns, he will come straight here. It's also possible I may have need of it."

"What could have happened?" Thierry asked anxiously.

"It is anybody's guess. Let us hope there is a simple explanation."

DeNarsac settled his helm and maneuvered his mount into position beside the long wooden barrier that divided the arena. His opponent was waiting at the far end.

The Marshal signaled he was ready to commence.

The drums began a long roll. The restless crowd became hushed and still.

Thierry placed an eleven-foot lance in DeNarsac's gloved hand. Looking through the narrow eyepiece of his helm, the knight concentrated on the challenger ahead of him. He was short and heavyset, and DeNarsac guessed there was much strength in his stocky frame.

"Lower lances!" the Marshal called. Looking left and right to ensure all was in order, he raised his right arm, then brought it down with a flourish.

"LAISSEZ ALLER!" he bellowed.

DeNarsac urged his mount into a canter, and the gray responded, gathering speed with every stride. Judging the distance and observing the posture of the knight coming toward him, DeNarsac swung the lance, settling it firmly in the notch of his shield and positioning it across his horse's neck. He had been right about the strength of his opponent. DeNarsac's lance connected with the knight's shoulder, but the blow did not unseat him. Nevertheless it was a hit, and the crowd shouted its approval.

Turning the gray at the far end of the lists, DeNarsac waited for his adversary to settle himself and began a second charge. This time neither man gained a hit, but now DeNarsac had the measure of the knight, and as he wheeled his mount for a third attempt, he knew what he should do. Sitting well into the saddle, he spurred the gray at the last moment to a greater speed, giving him a very slight edge. He thrust at the exact spot on the shoulder as before, and his lance splintered in all directions. Leaning away from the weapon aimed directly at him, DeNarsac experienced a glancing blow to his left arm. Well satisfied, he was proclaimed the winner, and he trotted back to the North Gate to much applause. The next two challengers took up their positions.

Thierry ran up to him. "*Bon sang!* That was well done!" he enthused as DeNarsac dismounted and removed his helmet.

"No word from Montdidier?"

"No, sir."

Richard Macaire was pitted against a knight of considerable fame—Josselin DuBois—and it was no accident that their contest was the centerpiece of the tournament: They had faced each other often and were well matched.

As he entered the lists, Macaire cut a grand figure. His black-and-gold armor was more elaborate than most, and its luster and detail were impressive against the white-and-gold caparison on his black stallion. Man and horse drew admiring cries from the populace, most especially the ladies. Enjoying the moment, Macaire indulged in a touch of impudence and showmanship, encouraging the huge destrier to rear in a marvelous display of power.

"Lower lances!" The Marshal raised his arm.

"LAISSEZ ALLER!"

Macaire allowed the nervous animal its head. Exploding into a gallop from the first stride, the horse unleashed its tremendous speed, muscular legs pounding and throwing up large clods of earth.

Josselin DuBois was barely able to stay in his saddle as Macaire's lance struck him a powerful blow and shattered to the hilt.

The crowd exploded with excitement. This was the kind of spectacle they had hoped to see. Thierry had been watching from a good vantage point, and he gave such a shout of enthusiasm that it brought DeNarsac to his side.

Macaire began his second pass, but DuBois, aware now of the speed and strength of his adversary, managed a speedy run of his own. He obtained a hit, albeit not a spectacular one. Though Macaire knew of his opponent's talent and ability, he was charged with a fierce excitement and ignored his better instincts. Spurring his mount, he charged into the third run without taking a moment for thought.

DeNarsac murmured, "Caution, caution . . ." and Thierry sucked in his breath sharply.

Josselin DuBois was a knowledgeable and courageous knight. Instead of being shaken by Macaire's first, blistering attack, he was cool and utterly focused. As men and horses met, his lance found its mark, hitting Macaire in the very center of his breastplate. The impact of DuBois's calculated thrust against the speed and strength of the Chevalier's ill-conceived assault threw Macaire backward and toppled him sideways to the ground. His foot twisted in its stirrup, and as the crowd rose to its feet in horror and dismay, Macaire was bounced and dragged behind the black stallion as it cantered down the lists.

Squires and pages, groundsmen and knights, including DeNarsac, ran onto the field, waving their arms at the horse. It slowed upon seeing the wall of men ahead, and DeNarsac caught its bridle, bringing the creature to a halt. Thierry felt sick at heart. As attendants arrived with a litter, he heard the wail that came from Macaire's mother and glimpsed Isabelle's concerned face. It seemed that the events of the day were tumbling one upon the other, too fast.

DeNarsac leaned down to his friend.

"God's mercy, Richard!"

Macaire gasped with pain. "I'm a *fool*," he whispered harshly. "This should have been my day."

Hysterical and tearful, Béatrice rushed down from the pavilion to be with her son as he was carried off the field and taken to the hospice in the château.

The tournament continued, and still there was no sign of Aubrey de Montdidier. Thierry could see that DeNarsac was now deeply concerned. The boy knew that only something catastrophic could have prevented the fair knight from participating in the joust, and he anxiously wondered what that might be. An accident, perhaps? Had his horse stumbled, broken a leg, thrown its rider? Could robbers have waylaid him on his morning ride or kidnapped him for ransom?

Gilbert and a groom arrived with Montdidier's chestnut destrier. When it became inevitable that DeNarsac would have to joust in his friend's place, he elected to use Montdidier's horse, saving his own gray for the last bout of the tournament, should that become necessary.

Grasping the pommel of the saddle, he swung in one easy movement onto the fresher mount and rode out to meet his new challenger. DeNarsac was horseman enough not be daunted by an unfamiliar steed, and the animal sensed he was being controlled by a strong rider. It was by no means an easy joust, but after a series of wrenching blows DeNarsac won by a narrow margin.

Now he was in the unenviable position of possibly having to play twice more. As the winner of his first tilt, he had to ride against the winner of the second, but, if successful, he would then face Josselin DuBois in the final round. Fate decreed this to be the case.

Thierry's heart pounded as he watched DeNarsac wearily remount his own destrier and, with Gilbert at his side, head to the lists for the final confrontation of the day. The odds were in DuBois's favor. The two knights were equally skilled, but DeNarsac had already been heavily taxed.

"Lower lances!"

Gilbert said encouragingly, "Trust the gray, sir. He

will not fail you." DeNarsac nodded.

The Marshal raised his arm for the last time, and the audience became tense and still.

"LAISSEZ ALLER!"

DeNarsac held back his expectant mount a second longer than usual and watched as DuBois began his run. The other knight was carrying his lance high, and DeNarsac made a calculated guess that he was going to thrust from shoulder height for more leverage. If DeNarsac aimed low, his helm would be vulnerable, so he decided to aim even higher than his opponent. He brought his lance down at the last possible moment to avoid revealing his intention. It was a dangerous gamble, and the timing was critical. The knights came together with tremendous impact, their lances locking one above the other. Both shattered spectacularly, gaining each man an equal hit.

DeNarsac took a deep breath as he received a new lance from Gilbert. Beginning his second run, he mentally targeted DuBois's shield, which the knight had raised in anticipation of a blow similar to the first. DeNarsac was mere yards away when DuBois's destrier suddenly missed its footing. The crowd gasped. DeNarsac raised his lance swiftly and swung his horse wide, allowing the disadvantaged knight to brush past without incident.

The throng yelled its appreciation for his chivalrous gesture. Now, with only a single pass remaining, one knight would have to joust superlatively in order to win the tournament. Thierry sent up a silent prayer to his favorite saint, Martin of Tours, and promised extra rosaries for good measure if he would look kindly upon his weary hero.

DeNarsac braced himself for the final run. Trusting his mount as he had been urged to do, he allowed the gray to pace itself. As it reached full stride, DeNarsac settled back against the cantle of the saddle for added stability and angled his lance low, then thrust upward with all his might. DuBois's helm was caught under the rim, and it flew from his head, arcing skyward and flashing in the sun as it tumbled to earth.

The ovation was deafening. Thierry sank to his knees, weak with relief and gratitude. DeNarsac turned his gray, acknowledged DuBois with a respectful salute, and rode slowly back toward the pavilion, where Isabelle, the Count, and their guests were standing and applauding.

Excited spectators broke through the barricades and stormed the field. Thierry elbowed his way through the crowd, reaching DeNarsac in time to relieve him of his lance.

"Montdidier could *not* have done better!" the boy gasped proudly.

A flock of white doves was released, fluttering and drifting like blossoms in the wind.

Thierry glanced at Isabelle, and suddenly the commotion, the sounds and sensations of the day, receded in his consciousness, to be replaced with concern. Her troubled face was whiter than the flurry of birds dipping and soaring above her.

Chapter Three
THE DISCOVERY

HE FESTIVITIES OF THE tournament continued
for two more days, but Isabelle and DeNarsac
did not attend, concentrating instead on the
search for Aubrey de Montdidier. His valet had been
unsuccessful in his attempt to locate the missing knight,
and the Count of Montargis ordered every available man
to participate in the hunt.

Together, DeNarsac and Thierry went into the village and inquired at lodgings. They walked by the banks
of the river and combed the bypaths and trails that
Montdidier loved to frequent on his morning rides.
Emissaries were sent to neighboring towns to investigate
whether anyone had seen or heard of his being in the
vicinity.

Thierry marveled at DeNarsac's calm demeanor

under such worrying circumstances, and he tried to emulate the knight's manner, even as his mind was teeming with visions of Montdidier being subjected to agonizing and dreadful horrors.

Isabelle spoke with the staff in the château, trying to glean information that might prove useful. She spent time with Aubrey's parents, the Count and Countess of Montdidier, gently encouraging them to remain optimistic. She busied herself with trivial tasks, longing to stem her own anxieties. But it was difficult—for it seemed that the knight, his horse, and his dog had vanished without a trace.

DeNarsac and Thierry visited Macaire in the hospice. Amazingly, he had sustained no broken bones from his accident, but had severely pulled a groin muscle, which limited his mobility. He was grateful for any news they brought him and equally concerned about Montdidier.

In a private moment he confided to DeNarsac.

"I have no wish to add to our worries, but my men and I had two encounters with marauders *en route* to Montargis. We dispatched them easily enough, but one man alone could not have managed. We also heard of a boar rampaging near Châteauneuf-sur-Loire. It attacked several dogs and a young shepherd. . . ."

DeNarsac kept the information to himself. But apprehension and rumor festered like an angry wound in the halls and chambers of the château.

On the evening of the third day, just after vespers, Thierry was attending to his final tasks before retiring for the night. Carrying a pallet of straw from the Count's chambers to the stables, he picked his way carefully across the dark courtyard. The moon was almost hidden and a ground mist floated above the cobblestones, giving the quadrangle an eerie, unearthly appearance.

Thierry wondered if Montdidier was out there somewhere, alone in the night, lost, frightened. Was he lying hurt, cold, desperate for someone to find him?

He was jarred from his reverie by an unfamiliar sound—something scraping on the cobblestones nearby. Before he could draw breath, an apparition loomed before him, shaking him to the core.

It was a horse . . . riderless, ghostlike, steam rising from its flanks.

It was Montdidier's palfrey.

The wild-eyed animal balked at sight of him and backed away.

"*Tiens, mon brave!* Stay. . . ." Thierry spoke soothingly to the trembling creature. Gently taking hold of the reins, he led it into the stables. He knew he should impart this news to Lady Isabelle but suddenly realized that DeNarsac's quarters were mere yards away, by the main gate. He hurried up the stone steps to his rooms and breathlessly knocked on the door.

"Mother of God, lad! You look as if you have seen a ghost!" DeNarsac said at sight of him.

Thierry gasped, "I thought I had!" and relayed what had just transpired.

DeNarsac ushered him inside and handed him a beaker of wine.

"What can this mean?" Thierry asked as he gulped it down.

"The horse found his way home. He cannot have been too far away." DeNarsac poured himself a beaker. "It means tomorrow we must double our efforts."

"Should I tell her ladyship?"

"Has she retired for the night?"

"Yes."

"Let us not worry her at this hour. There is nothing we can do until daybreak." Noting the boy's pallor, DeNarsac added, "Would you care to rest here tonight? You can take that pallet in the corner."

Thierry nodded, grateful. It took him a long time to settle, and he tossed and turned restlessly. Where had Montdidier's horse been for the past three days? Why and how had he become separated from his master? Did it mean that Montdidier had fallen and was suffering—or worse? Listening to DeNarsac breathing deeply and evenly, he wished that he, too, could sleep.

He wondered what hour it was. The room was dark and silent.

A board creaked.

Was it a board? Yes. But surely the night air was making the wood contract. The wine was playing with his senses.

Something scuffed against the door.

Thierry lay rigid, not daring to breathe. He heard the sound again and sat bolt upright—only to discover that DeNarsac was sitting up also, holding up his hand for silence.

Nothing. And then a soft cry.

Sword at the ready, DeNarsac was across the room in two strides. He flung open the door.

There was a dark shape, crouched, whining.

It was Dragon.

DeNarsac dropped to his knees.

"Thierry, we need light," he whispered urgently.

Thierry found the tinderbox. With trembling fingers, he lit a taper and touched it to the tallow-dipped head of an iron torch.

Dragon was revealed in the flickering light, shivering, bleeding, his fur matted with mud and leaves.

DeNarsac ran outside and down the steps, hoping that Montdidier was there—but not a soul was in sight. Returning, he gently led Dragon to Thierry's pallet and said, "Fetch water . . . and meat."

Thierry stumbled across the dark courtyard and into the pantry. Grabbing a slab of smoked venison, he ran to the well and filled a bowl, his thoughts cascading as fast as the water spilling over his shaking hands. Trying not to waste too much, he hastened back to the guardhouse.

It was obvious that Dragon had had no sustenance, for he drank deeply and gobbled the small pieces that

Thierry tore from the meat. DeNarsac dipped a cloth in the remaining liquid and gently cleansed the dog.

He hissed sharply as the wounds became evident.

"*Mon Dieu!* These are knife cuts," he exclaimed. "See how clean, how precise?"

A look passed between the man and the boy.

Thierry curled up on the pallet beside the dog. Dragon was racked with tremors and lay on his side, eyes wide, his breath rasping. The boy stroked him and gently picked leaves and mud from his coat.

Eventually, he drifted into fitful slumber.

There was just a hint of light in the sky when the dog sighed and raised his head. Moments later, he rose unsteadily to his feet, shook himself, and whined gently.

Thierry and DeNarsac awakened simultaneously.

Dragon padded stiffly to the door and looked at them.

DeNarsac murmured, "Go with him, Thierry; then bring him back and we will rest a little longer."

Thierry wearily got up and opened the door, murmuring to the dog to follow him. Dragon hesitated, whined once again, and walked back into the room to sit at DeNarsac's side.

"Dragon. Come!" Thierry urged.

The dog placed a paw on DeNarsac's bed. The knight sleepily opened his eyes.

"What is it, good fellow?" he asked.

Dragon walked two paces and looked back at him.

Yawning, DeNarsac sat up and rubbed his head. "Surely the devil is playing with us this night," he groaned. "Very well, Dragon. Go to. We will all step outside together."

They went down the steps into the courtyard. It was barely dawn, and all was still.

Dragon went to the stone archway and stood, waiting.

"Does he wish us to follow?" Thierry asked in surprise.

"It would seem so." DeNarsac hesitated, then walked several paces toward the dog. Dragon moved on, only to stop and look back again.

"Yes, Thierry, that is exactly what he wishes. But we should take the horses. Who knows how far he may lead us?" He called softly, "Hold, Dragon," and hurried to the stables, Thierry at his side.

The dawn chorus was in full-throated glory and the tip of an orange sun was just emerging as the knight and the boy rode out from the château.

Dragon was waiting for them, and now he limped ahead, leading them across the river bridge, through the sleeping village, and out into the open countryside, pausing only to ensure that they were following.

Thierry's hands fussed with the reins, and his voice shook. "Where is he taking us? What does he want?"

"We will know soon enough."

The dog took a bypath heading toward the Forest of Bondy. Soon they entered the shadow of the green canopy.

As they rode beneath the boughs of the trees, DeNarsac remarked quietly, "This does not bode well," and Thierry noticed that he placed a hand lightly upon his sword. The horses plodded silently across the forest's mossy carpet. A startled bird flapped over their heads, shrieking a warning, and Thierry's heart missed a beat. Dragon pressed deeper and deeper into the trees, until they came to a huge and ancient oak, its roots gnarled and thick, its spreading limbs almost touching the ground.

Dragon halted, then approached a low mound of earth and dead leaves. Whimpering, he lay down on top of it, his head on his paws.

DeNarsac reined his horse and dismounted. Signaling for Thierry to stay where he was, he walked to the dog and knelt beside him. Dragon looked at him, his eyes dark and unblinking. The knight took up a handful of earth, letting it sift through his fingers, and brushed the leaves with an open palm. Solemnly, he made the sign of the cross, then rose and walked back to Thierry. The boy saw that he was choked with emotion, and he knew intuitively what DeNarsac was about to say.

"I fear that Dragon has led us to his master. It is my guess that Montdidier is buried here."

Thierry nodded, fighting a rush of tears. "What should we do?" he asked.

DeNarsac glanced about him worriedly. "We need help. Do you think you could ride back to the château without me? I should stay, for I know that Dragon will not leave this spot again, and whoever committed this atrocity may return."

"I will do it, gladly," Thierry said.

"Bring Gilbert and several others back with you. We

will need tools and also a litter . . . and Thierry, ride with all possible speed. Do not stop for anyone or anything. Do you understand?"

"Yes, sir. What should I tell Lady Isabelle?"

DeNarsac threw back his head. "God in Heaven! Tell her . . . we must try to be gentle . . . tell her that we are not yet certain. The signs are not good, but she will be the first to hear upon our return."

"Yes, sir. Will you be safe while I am gone?"

"I will be safe. I have Dragon." DeNarsac smiled, attempting to allay the boy's concern. "Now go quickly— and may the Lord be with you."

Thierry wheeled his horse, spurring him to a canter, guiding him, twisting and turning through the trees. The leaves scraped his face as he ducked beneath the low branches. He prayed that he would find his way out of the forest without getting lost. Was this the same path as before? Yes, for there was the small gully he had noticed. But which direction should he now take? He glanced up at the sunlight filtering through the leaves overhead and swung his horse to the right.

What was that shape? Only the remains of a splintered tree. Was someone in the branches above, waiting to jump? No, that was just a twisted bough. He dared not look behind, for he felt as though all the demons in the world were chasing after him.

He burst from the forest into light so dazzling that he was momentarily blinded. But he breathed more easily now and settled to the rhythm of his horse. Boy and beast were as one, racing across the plain toward the château.

As Thierry clattered into the courtyard, he was barely able to contain his sobs, and he called Gilbert's name repeatedly.

The squire came running from the stables.

"We think we have found him!" Thierry gasped. "Buried in the forest! We need help!" He relayed DeNarsac's instructions and was grateful when the young man immediately understood and took charge. Thierry dismounted and led his horse to water, then slaked his own thirst and splashed his face. He was shaking violently. Everything seemed unreal. For a moment he wondered if he was suffering another nightmare. But as he took bread from the pantry and wrapped meat and wine in a scarf for DeNarsac, he knew this was not a dream, and was calmed by the reality of the simple chore.

* * *

Barely two hours later, Thierry rode out ahead of the party, retracing the path he had taken earlier in the day. As they neared the huge oak tree, he called for DeNarsac and was relieved to hear an answering cry.

The knight came to greet them. Touching Thierry's shoulder, he said, "You did well. Now distract Dragon while we do what we have to do."

The dog seemingly had not moved. But he growled and curled his lip as the men approached. Thierry went to him and twined his fingers in the fur of his neck.

"Come, good fellow," he said encouragingly. "They only wish to help."

Dragon reluctantly allowed Thierry to lead him away. The boy sat on a root of the oak tree, his arms encircling the dog, and watched as the men began their dismal task.

With spade and fork they labored until, as DeNarsac had predicted, the body of Montdidier was unearthed. Thierry buried his face in Dragon's side and wept as the corpse was gently lifted from its shallow grave. He heard the men exclaim angrily. Glancing up, he was devastated by what he saw.

Aubrey de Montdidier, the once-beautiful knight, had been brutally stabbed several times. His face was muddied, and maggots had already invaded his eyes, hair, and bloodied wounds. The effect was grotesque, and gave substance to Thierry's ever-present imaginings of another tragedy—the butchery of his parents. Nausea clutched at the boy's stomach, and he ran behind the tree to retch until there was nothing left to bring up. Flushed and dripping with sweat, he slid to his knees.

DeNarsac was at his side, his hand on Thierry's shoulder.

"I'm sorry," the boy gasped.

"There is nothing to be ashamed of."

Montdidier's body was gently placed upon a horse-drawn litter. There was a piece of cloth knotted around the fallen knight's arm. Once cornflower blue, it was now soaked with blood and caked with earth.

Thierry whispered, "My lady's kerchief . . ." and wept once more.

Removing the favor, DeNarsac covered the body with his cloak and some fresh green boughs. The party began the slow, sorrowful journey out of the forest.

The sky had become leaden with dark clouds, and shadows swept across the plain. The men lit torches, and they flickered in the wind. Barely a word was spoken as the solemn procession headed for the château.

Dragon padded along close to his fallen master. Thierry rode beside the dog, glancing occasionally at the litter and its heartbreaking cargo. He felt drained and deeply weary. He glanced ahead to DeNarsac, who was hunched in his saddle, deep in thought.

There was a low rumble of thunder.

Isabelle came running from the château gates toward them. DeNarsac swung to the ground and caught her as she tried to reach Montdidier.

"It is better that you don't, Milady . . ."

"I will see him," she said fiercely. "I *must*!"

She broke from his grasp and ran to the litter, pulling back the cloak to reveal her beloved's ravaged face. Thierry would forever remember the sound that escaped from her throat, from her very soul. The strength draining from her body, she swayed and fell to embrace the lifeless form.

Thunder and lightning split open the sky and the deluge began, staining the baked earth.

Thierry was choked with grief. It seemed that even the heavens were weeping.

Chapter Four

THE FAREWELL

EWS OF MONTDIDIER'S HEINOUS murder spread quickly, and the château and its community were blanketed in mourning.

Montdidier's anguished parents were persuaded by the Count of Montargis to bury their son in the family cemetery at the château, where he would be accorded every honor and dignity.

The knight was bathed with perfumed water and rubbed with ointments and balsam. Dressed in the finest clothing, his body was laid out in the chancel of the church before the stone altar, draped with a shroud of pure linen, then surrounded by summer grasses and flowers. Candlesticks were placed at either side of the bier, their flickering flames illuminating the still-vibrant sheen of the knight's golden hair. A tall cross stood at his head, another at his feet. Two monks kept a silent vigil.

The family visited privately in the hours before the funeral service. Isabelle never left Montdidier's side. Clutching the bloodied blue scarf that DeNarsac had returned to her, she stayed in the chapel throughout the night. For hours, she alternately stroked her beloved's brow or kissed his hand, whispering endearments, sobs racking her body. Concerned for her welfare, Thierry remained with her, wishing he could offer comfort, that he could embrace her slight frame and infuse her with strength. But he was struggling with his own anguish. Though he, too, longed for consolation, he kept a respectful distance, afraid that his own tears would stress her more.

The church bell tolled as nobles, friends, retainers, and villagers filed into the cold, damp chapel. Incense hung in the air; the priest intoned a Latin dirge. The grieving family arrived and the congregation rose to acknowledge them.

The Count led the procession, Isabelle at his side, holding his arm for support, her lovely face the color of alabaster beneath her gossamer veil. Thierry followed behind, head bowed. The Count and Countess of Montdidier came next, then Béatrice with her son, Macaire, who walked slowly and painfully on crutches. When DeNarsac had informed him of Montdidier's death, Macaire had been disbelieving, then distraught, weeping unashamedly. He had insisted upon attending the service, even though he should not have left his bed. Lieutenant Landry hovered at his shoulder, followed by DeNarsac. The steward of the château and several dignitaries brought up the rear.

The service was simple: A mass was said, the Count gave a eulogy, hymns were sung, and Father Benedict, the Count's uncle and confessor, delivered a sermon. Afterward the family stood outside, accepting condolences as the guests filed past. Thierry watched as Isabelle graciously acknowledged everyone. Her eyes were luminous, but she shed no more tears. She greeted Macaire tenderly and was solicitous for his well-being. Béatrice was uncharacteristically silent.

The burial itself was restricted to the family and household staff. Montdidier's body was taken by the monks and sewn into a deerskin shroud. As it was placed in a coffin inscribed with the Montdidier coat of arms, Thierry whispered a final good-bye to his noble friend who had been the epitome of chivalry, decency, and honor. The monks carried the coffin slowly to the cemetery, accompanied by the mourners.

Macaire said quietly, "The weeks ahead will be difficult for Isabelle. We must all support her. It is the least we can do for Aubrey."

DeNarsac nodded. "Thierry and I will see her daily. You must visit often, Richard."

"I intend to. His Majesty has summoned me to Paris—I know not why. I must leave tomorrow if I can obtain a suitable wagon. But if you have need of me, you have only to send word."

The guests departed, the daily rituals were taken up once again, and a semblance of normalcy began to return, though life for the inhabitants of the château would never be quite the same.

Two summer moons came and went. Harvesting began.

Thierry was not yet aware that the recent tragedy had stolen from him a certain innocence. He felt deeply sad.

Sleep was elusive, and when he did slumber, he was tormented by his old nightmares. He stumbled through his daily chores, barely aware of his actions. Every free moment was spent with DeNarsac, for he found solace in the good man's company.

Dragon seemed also to be in mourning. He, too, stayed near DeNarsac, sleeping at the foot of his bed, sitting at his side in the great hall, his wounds healing but still discernible. The knight went about his duties, more often than not followed closely by the boy and the dog, as if they were his shadows. He tolerated them with understanding, though he was often preoccupied with his own melancholy thoughts.

Isabelle stayed mostly in seclusion, wrestling with her grief. But she was not oblivious to Thierry's sorrowful mien, and one evening, seated before her bedroom mirror, she called to him.

"Would you attend to my hair for me?" she asked, handing him her brush.

"Of course, Milady."

It was a small ritual they had often enjoyed together. Rhythmically, evenly, he stroked her long, fair tresses.

Isabelle said, "Thierry, two months have passed and I

have not seen you smile."

"No, Milady."

"I confess I have missed that," she observed gently. "True, there has been no cause for joy and my heart has also been heavy, but perhaps we need to encourage each other at this time."

"Oh, Milady, I can endure. But I am concerned about you."

"Well—then we are both concerned. You are so much wiser than your years, and these past months you have shown much strength. But do not be so strong that you ignore the wonder that life still has to offer you."

Thierry felt his throat constrict. It was difficult to speak, and he stammered, "I will try. Will *you* try?"

But she rose from her seat, seeming not to have heard him.

Word came from Macaire. He was unable to return to Montargis, having been promoted by the King to be his new Captain of the Guard—the position once held by Montdidier.

Macaire wrote, *"This is difficult for me and has occurred at a painful time—yet how does one refuse His Majesty? I can never replace my cousin. I pray that I may execute my duties capably and, in so doing, honor his memory.*" He inquired after Isabelle's health and sent warm greetings, promising to visit at the first opportunity.

The high days of summer melted into autumn. DeNarsac was busy on the Count's behalf, and Thierry took over some of the tasks concerning Dragon's care. The boy and the dog had bonded closer. Thierry delighted in Dragon's quick intelligence, his obedience, his lively sense of play. The dog instinctively knew what was expected of him—when to be respectful, when to remain patient, when it was permissible to romp, gambol, nuzzle.

Thierry and Gilbert often rode together in the cool, misty mornings, Dragon at their side. They avoided the forest, partly because the memory of what had happened there was still fresh, but also because DeNarsac had given them explicit instructions to stay near the château and to remain in each other's company. The people of Montargis had come to believe that Montdidier had been slain by thieves or marauders, and DeNarsac was concerned that those persons might still be in the vicinity.

No matter how busy they were, Thierry and

DeNarsac kept their vow to care for Isabelle's well-being. In his quiet way, DeNarsac sustained her through the darkest days of her grief, and her presence eased the heaviness he continued to feel.

One afternoon, he found her sitting with Thierry beneath a tree in the cemetery garden, giving the boy his Latin instruction. DeNarsac paused, enjoying the picture of the two, their heads close as they turned the pages of the book. Dragon broke the moment by bounding up to them, and Thierry caught him in his arms and hugged him. They fell back on the grass, and the dog licked his face.

"Apologies for disturbing you, Milady."

"We were almost finished. Thierry welcomes the interruption, I am sure."

Thierry scrambled to his feet and threw a stick for Dragon, who went loping after it.

DeNarsac continued, "I have come with news, Milady. I must depart for Paris tomorrow. Your father wishes the steward to prepare the house in the city, and he requests that I, and some of the guard, escort him and provide our services."

Isabelle stood and brushed the leaves from her gown.

"I understand. How long will you be gone?"

"No more than a week, I would imagine. I am hoping to see Macaire. Do you wish me to carry a letter to him?"

"Perhaps," she said absently.

"Is there something I may do for you while I am away?" asked DeNarsac.

"Yes, possibly." She turned to him, and he thought that her eyes resembled the color of the wild violets he had seen in a field that morning. "Would you take Thierry with you?"

Thierry looked at DeNarsac, then back to Isabelle. "But Milady—I could not leave. I—how would you . . . no, no, it is impossible."

"Thierry, it is very possible. You will soon be fourteen years old, and in truth you are ready to begin your apprenticeship as a knight. I know you have long hoped to be a certain someone's squire"—she smiled at DeNarsac, who immediately understood—"and what better way to prove your worth than by assisting him in Paris? Besides, a change of scenery will do you good."

Thierry's thoughts were tumbling, spinning. "But Milady, this is not the time. Not *now*. . . ." He turned to

DeNarsac imploringly. "You know what I mean. Please tell her. Anyway," he added lamely, "who will look after Dragon?"

"I am perfectly capable of looking after Dragon," Isabelle said spiritedly. "In fact it is a splendid idea. He will protect me while you are gone. We will care for each other, won't we, my friend?" The dog wagged his tail as she caressed him.

DeNarsac chuckled. "It seems you are outnumbered, Thierry. I agree with her ladyship and would welcome your company. For good measure, I shall ask Gilbert to stay behind. He will help with Dragon. So all you have to do is say yes."

"Oh. Well . . . *mon Dieu*! Well! Then—then yes!" Thierry felt as if a weight had been lifted from his shoulders, and he felt happier than he had in months.

Chapter Five

THE MÊLÉE

ARIS HAD CHANGED MUCH since Thierry was last there. Or was it that he had changed, he wondered? Before, he had always visited as page to Isabelle. Now he was a young man among men. From the moment he passed the ancient abbey of Saint-Germain-des-Prés and saw the immense barrier of the city walls and the roofs, spires, and chimneys, he was enthralled with the wonder of it all.

The great metropolis was abustle with activity: travelers, merchants, monks, beggars, street peddlers, washerwomen. There were elegant nobles with wide-brimmed hats. Soldiers of the King's Guard pressed their horses through the crowded lanes, and children played in the muddy streets. Shops displayed their wares: goldsmiths, bookbinders, weavers, tailors—and a glimpse inside the stores revealed the floors strewn with fresh rushes, and apprentices bent to their tasks.

After the tranquility of Montargis, the noise was overwhelming. Bells rang constantly, oxen hauled rattling carts that carried bales of wool, sacks of grain, bundles of skins, and wood. Vendors hawked wine and fish, bread and vegetables. Dogs barked and geese ran underfoot, honking their alarm.

Thierry's nose was assaulted by odors: sewage and waste ran in gutters down the muddy roads, and refuse from butcher shops and fish markets rotted where it lay. But there were wonderful scents as well—fresh-baked bread, spices, flowers and fruit, wood fires, and tantalizing aromas of food coming from the inns and taverns.

The Count of Montargis's Paris residence was in the newly developed part of the city—the Marais, on the Right Bank—and DeNarsac and Thierry were kept busy escorting the steward and his staff as they stocked the townhouse and put it in order. Every excursion gave Thierry a chance to glimpse something fresh, to learn something new.

DeNarsac went out of his way to show him things that would enlighten and entertain. He pointed out the flying buttresses and fascinating gargoyles of the great Cathedral of Notre Dame, the exquisite stained-glass windows of the Sainte-Chapelle, and the recently completed fortress of the Louvre, where the King was in residence.

He took Thierry to the Rue des Pelletiers and they watched the tanners stirring their foul-smelling cauldrons in which animal hides were boiled. They visited parchment makers who fashioned paper from sheepskin, and marveled at miniaturists who illustrated manuscripts with exquisite detail. DeNarsac identified moneylenders and tax collectors scurrying about the city in drab attire, ledgers clutched protectively to their chests. Thierry saw sculptors, painters, stonemasons, joiners, and glassmakers working on the numerous buildings springing up all over the city. With each day that passed, the boy's mood brightened.

It was only on the last evening of that exciting week in Paris that they were able to see Macaire. Arrangements were made to meet in a tavern, *Les Trois Rois*, situated near the university on the Left Bank of the Seine.

Their tasks complete for the day, DeNarsac and

Thierry rode toward the river. Dusk was falling, and as they came to the water's edge, it was a picture of serenity—anglers fishing, boatmen mooring their craft for the night. Two barges coming in late from the countryside plowed slowly upstream to the docks, one laden with barrels of wine, the other with a cargo of salt.

Turning right onto the towpath, the riders came to the establishment with the gaily painted sign of The Three Kings. Macaire had not yet arrived, but DeNarsac and Thierry secured a good table, and the young man's mouth was agape as he took in the colorful scene. Torches had been lit for the evening. The walls were hung with tapestries and artifacts—scepters, a falchion, shields and lances. There was an intoxicating smell—a mixture of cooked meats, tallow, sawdust, sweat, and stale spirits. Goblets of wine were being balanced on a huge platter by a young serving girl, and the brawny owner of the establishment carried several tankards of foaming ale in his beefy hands, setting them in front of his customers, barely spilling a drop.

A pair of elderly men sat at a corner table playing chess, paying no heed to a group of rowdy students nearby. A juggler performed for the crowd, and Thierry remarked that he would like to learn the skill and surprise Isabelle and the Count when they returned home.

Macaire hailed them from the doorway. He was walking with a cane, but he embraced DeNarsac heartily and gave Thierry a little punch of pleasure. His eyes were sparkling with delight.

"*Vraiment*, it's good to see you!" He beamed. "Sorry to be late." He caught the young serving girl by the waist as she passed. "Wench, we will have ale, if you please."

DeNarsac added quickly, "And wine, watered, for the young man."

Macaire winked at Thierry. "What a good uncle he is! The evening is young, and we have hours to enjoy ourselves. *Quel plaisir!*"

Thierry noted, "You look in good health, Macaire. Is your leg healing well?"

"It catches me from time to time, but as you see I am without my crutches." He spun around, demonstrating his agility, then seated himself on the bench opposite them. "Now—I want news. I am thirsty for news . . . and ale!" He thumped the table impatiently.

"You first!" chuckled DeNarsac. "Tell us everything. How you fare . . . your duties . . ."

"Do you see the King often?" Thierry asked.

"Indeed I do. I see him many times during the week. There is always some function, some excursion that requires my presence."

"What is he like?"

"Quiet. An intellectual. An ascetic, almost. He loves his library, loves art, loves to build. You must see the château at Vincennes now that it is finished. It is quite spectacular."

"Has your mother paid you a visit?" Thierry grinned wickedly.

Macaire looked at him sideways and raised an eyebrow. "What do *you* think? I can hardly keep her away."

"So this is a pleasant posting?" DeNarsac inquired.

"Now? Yes. But it has not been easy." Macaire leaned forward, his elbows on the table. "I wrote you that His Majesty could not have asked for me at a more difficult time. To walk so soon in Montdidier's shoes, to live in the quarters that he occupied, to see his possessions, to command his men . . ." His voice trailed off as their drinks arrived, and he took a large swallow of ale. Wiping his mouth, he repeated, quietly, "No. It has not been easy."

"Though certainly it is an honor," DeNarsac put in.

"And who better to succeed Aubrey than you?"

"I suppose I was the natural successor—rather obvious, since I am also a relative," Macaire conceded drily.

"I was thinking more about your ability, Richard. His Majesty was correct to ask you."

"Thank you." Macaire looked downcast for a moment, then shifted his mood abruptly. "So. How is my beautiful Isabelle? *Par Dieu,* I miss her!"

"She is better than she was," Thierry offered, "but I wonder if she will ever put the tragedy behind her. The village seems so quiet these days. . . ."

". . . Which is one of the reasons Thierry came to Paris with me," DeNarsac added cheerily. "This visit came at a welcome time."

"Well, I certainly welcome it!" Macaire drained his tankard and called, "Landlord! Another round, if you please!"

The students, who had been playing dice, began a rousing song—and for a moment everyone in the tavern turned to listen to them, with the exception of the two elderly chess players, who were still too absorbed in their game.

Macaire said, "These university lads revel every night. I presume there is little else that pleases them so much. Speaking of which," he added, "are you aware that in four weeks His Majesty will host his annual Feast of Saint Martin?"

DeNarsac nodded. "That is why we are preparing the house in the Marais. I am told that the Count has received an invitation."

"He has!" Thierry confirmed. "Isabelle showed it to me. It's very grand. The entire Montargis family has been invited."

"Splendid! Then I will be seeing you again soon." Macaire lifted his tankard in salutation and drank deeply. "Isabelle will come, of course?"

DeNarsac shook his head. "I suspect that she will not."

"But she must!" Macaire slapped his mug on the table. "This is a perfect opportunity for her to take up her life once again."

"I *know* she will not come," Thierry said. "You haven't seen her, Macaire. She is still distraught."

Macaire's eyes darkened for a moment.

"Then we must construct a plan to help her! We

must implore her, woo her, beg her!" He became suddenly excited. "You shall take my letter to her, Guy. I will write that I am desolate—which is the truth, Lord knows—and that she is being too unkind to this cousin who misses her so desperately." Macaire giggled as he warmed to the idea. "You must go on bended knee if necessary to aid our cause, and you, Thierry, must influence her in every way you can. We are rescuing a beautiful damsel who cannot know what is best for her."

Thierry nodded, fired by his enthusiasm. "We could try, I suppose." He looked at DeNarsac. "What do *you* think?"

The knight glanced over at the students, who were singing lustily.

"I will gladly take your letter, Richard," he said. "I, too, believe it would help Lady Isabelle to come to Paris, but I very much doubt that she will."

Macaire called for yet another order of drinks.

DeNarsac said quickly, "I have not finished mine—and Thierry still has half a glass."

Macaire leaned back and stretched his legs.

"Ahh. It is good to relax. You cannot imagine the pressure at Court. I complained about the garrison, I know, but here there is so much protocol. And one is seldom acknowledged for one's efforts."

The serving girl brought his ale, and he pulled her onto his lap.

"You are a pretty one!" He gave her a dazzling smile. "Do you have lodgings in the vicinity?"

"I live upstairs," she replied. Indicating the landlord, she added tartly, "And *that* is my father."

DeNarsac exploded with laughter, and Thierry felt the blood surge to his cheeks as Macaire hurriedly pushed her away. The knight gulped his ale and said ruefully, "I told you these are difficult times. My Lieutenant, Landry, has more opportunity for pleasure than I do. There is precious little freedom for a Captain of the King's Guard."

The students were now disputing loudly.

Macaire suddenly yelled, "For love of Sainte Geneviève! A person cannot *think* with such a commotion!"

A pale-faced lad with a poor complexion sauntered over to their table.

"Haven't we seen you here before?"

Macaire ignored him and drained his tankard.

"*Monsieur!* I am talking to you."

DeNarsac said evenly, "We are here to enjoy our evening, sirrah, as are you. Shall we allow one another to do just that?"

Another student joined them. He noticed Thierry and said, "Boy, you look too young to hold your wine. Where are you from?"

"Montargis, sir," Thierry replied.

"Country folk! I thought as much!"

The first student called to the others, "Friends! We have distinguished visitors from the provinces."

"Uneducated, and with no manners!" One more youth joined the group, beckoning to his companions to follow.

Macaire did not look up, but his face was flushed. "There are more good men in Montargis than in your chapel on the Sabbath," he growled.

DeNarsac placed a hand lightly on Macaire's arm. "Richard. No need to take offense. We are all good men—and *wise*," he added pointedly.

"No, by God." Macaire threw him off, as if to dislodge a pestering fly. "A whining, pockmarked novice should not address a knight in service to His Majesty with so little respect."

The students pressed closer.

"Respect is for those who command it!" a young man jeered.

Macaire took up a new tankard and said, loudly and deliberately, "What would an effete bookworm like you know about respect, chivalry, or *life*, for that matter?"

DeNarsac was grim faced. "Richard, I beg you . . ."

"Better an effete bookworm than a vulgar country lout." The first student came within an inch of Macaire's face. "What do you do for entertainment in Montargis, *monsieur* of the King's Guard? Butcher sheep?"

The entire tavern seemed to hold its breath. Macaire scraped back his bench. With a roar, he went for the student's throat.

The fight was on.

Macaire threw the young man against the wall. Two others jumped on his back. Ducking and twisting, he took them both over a table, which crashed to the ground. DeNarsac thrust himself in front of Thierry and said urgently, "Find a safe corner and *stay* there!" He deflected a blow from a youth who was upon him, giving him a swift, small punch that sent him reeling.

Macaire had now been taken down by several students, and DeNarsac hurled himself at them and peeled them off, one by one. Other customers joined the brawl, and food and ale flew in all directions. The landlord bellowed for everyone to stop, but no one took any notice. He took hold of an iron skillet and, swinging left and right, flattened several patrons.

Thierry tried to back away but found his path blocked by the mob of students, who were regrouping. He climbed onto a bench to avoid them. One young man lifted a wooden stool over his head and was preparing to use it on DeNarsac's skull. Thierry plucked it deftly out of his hand, then brought it down on the lad's own shoulders instead. No sooner had he done so than he was knocked from his perch by a tide of humanity. He found himself on his hands and knees in the wood shavings on the floor. Macaire's bloodied face loomed in front of him.

"What are you doing down here?" Macaire grinned. He rolled nimbly to one side as a falling body missed him by inches.

Thierry saw Macaire's cane lying under the table and crawled between several pairs of legs to retrieve it. Using it to parry and thrust his way up through the crush, he saw DeNarsac looking around, desperately trying to find him. He yelled, and the knight pushed through the sea of people, grabbed his hand, and dragged him toward the tavern door. They were accosted by the student who had begun the argument, now wielding the falchion that, moments earlier, had been hanging on the wall. The crowd parted hastily, allowing them room, and DeNarsac shook his head and resignedly drew his own sword.

Three swift strokes and the young man was disarmed. The falchion landed point downward, quivering in the wood of the bar.

His path clear, DeNarsac virtually threw Thierry outside the tavern door and waded back into the throng to find Macaire.

Thierry staggered to a bench by the wall and sat gripping the cane, his heart pounding. DeNarsac reappeared, shouldering a disheveled Macaire, who was singing happily. Thierry's smile turned to a cry of warning as a student ran up behind them, a broken bottle in his hand. Extending Macaire's cane, Thierry tripped him, and the student sprawled on the ground.

DeNarsac said, "Good lad. Where are the horses?"

"Over there!" Thierry pointed. "I don't know where

Macaire left his . . ."

"No matter. Come!" They stumbled to the tethered animals, and Thierry helped lift the drunken Macaire onto DeNarsac's mount. DeNarsac swung up behind to support him. Thierry climbed onto his rouncy, and with *Les Trois Rois* in pandemonium behind them, they rode with all haste to Macaire's barracks.

"You know, that was most interesting." Macaire spoke to no one in particular, his voice slurred. "We haven't sparred like that since we were young men, many, many moons ago. Mmm! Are you aware, Thierry, that we all grew up together and we loved one another very, very much? Isabelle, and Guy, and—and Aubrey, and I. I should write a verse about it."

DeNarsac said sharply, "You should sleep on it first, my friend."

They left him in the capable hands of a night watchman, who promised to deliver Macaire to his squire.

Riding home beneath a canopy of stars, DeNarsac and Thierry were silent, both reflecting on the disturbing turn the evening had taken.

Finally, DeNarsac said lightly, "I think it best not to

mention this little escapade to anyone."

Thierry nodded solemnly. "Especially Isabelle."

"Especially Isabelle!" DeNarsac chuckled. "Oh, you are growing up fast, my young squire. You handled yourself well this evening."

That night they slept the sleep of angels.

Chapter Six

THE INCIDENT

HEY RETURNED TO Montargis none the worse for the previous night's encounter. In fact, Thierry was lighter of heart, and both he and DeNarsac felt refreshed from their week in Paris.

DeNarsac carried a sealed letter from Macaire for Isabelle. It had been delivered by a messenger on the morning of their departure. In a separate note to DeNarsac and Thierry, Macaire had written:

"Concerning last evening: Forgive foolish behavior. Ale too green. Filled with remorse—Richard."

DeNarsac commented wryly that he hadn't expected to hear from Macaire at all, considering the amount of alcohol he had consumed.

Dragon was delighted to see his beloved friends. He pressed himself against them both, weaving about their legs and thumping them with his tail. He brought little gifts to lay at their feet—a ball, a bone, a slipper.

Isabelle was pleased also. Still in mourning and thinner than before, she listened with interest as they regaled her with details of their visit—excluding the incident at the tavern.

They gave her Macaire's letter, and she perused its contents by the light of a window. A small smile played across her face as she read, but when she had finished, she looked up at DeNarsac and her eyes were clouded.

"His words are kind," she said, "but I cannot possibly go to Paris. It is too soon for festivities."

DeNarsac searched for his own words. "Milady, no one can dispute the pain you feel at the loss of our dear friend Aubrey. But with great respect, have you asked yourself what *he* might wish for you now?"

She said irritably, "I *do* ask myself that question, Guy, but my mind is such that I receive no answers. I feel only confusion."

Thierry went to her and quietly took her hand in his.

DeNarsac said, "Madame, I am very clear about one point. Aubrey appreciated every moment of every day that he lived. He would want you to rejoice in what you had together, rather than mourn what you have lost." Isabelle seemed taken aback, and he worried he had overstepped the boundaries of friendship.

But she lowered her head and murmured, "I thank you for your concern and your thoughts." She lightly kissed Thierry's brow, and the sweet perfume of her lingered in the room after she had departed.

The Count of Montargis went hawking the following morning and asked DeNarsac and Thierry to join his party. Dragon loped beside the hunting spaniels as they excitedly and noisily headed for the river. The intention was to bag some ducks, and to that end the Count carried a magnificent peregrine falcon on his wrist.

The morning was autumnal, and tinges of gold and russet showed in the trees. The Count maneuvered his palfrey to ride beside DeNarsac and Thierry.

"I understand that the house in Paris is in good order," he said. "We shall depart for the royal festivities in two weeks, and will have a large retinue, since Béatrice has asked if her entourage can join ours. It is only because she desires help with her sot of a husband, who unfortunately will be attending the celebrations also."

Thierry suppressed a smile but said nothing.

"We will be spending our first evening *en route* at the Château Moret-sur-Loing and the night after that at the abbey at Vitry. You'll inform your men and the grooms."

"Yes, Milord."

The Count lowered his voice. "In truth, I am concerned about Isabelle," he confided. "She is loath to leave Montargis. I understand her reasons, but it is not every week one is invited to Court. I feel it is time for her to resume her filial duties."

DeNarsac nodded. "I attempted to speak with her about this yesterday, but I believe Montdidier's death is still too painful for her."

The Count said moodily, "This whole business has thrown a shadow over us all. Isabelle grieves so much that I fear sorrow will shortly become her way of life."

"I know you would not wish to press her too harshly on the subject," DeNarsac said tactfully.

"No, no, of course not. I do try to respect her wishes. If only my dear Eleanor were alive, she would know what to do. It would be so much easier for Isabelle to be counseled by a woman. Whatever I say seems wrong," he added morosely.

They rode in silence for a while; then DeNarsac said, "Could you perhaps suggest that she talk with Father Benedict? He is a decent man of God and has particularly good insight into the ways of humankind."

The Count brightened. "That is a splendid idea. *Merci, mon ami.* I shall mention it to Isabelle at an appropriate moment."

The Count's falconer approached them. "Milord, the dogs are ready. Do you wish to unhood the falcon, or would you prefer to wait?"

"No, by all means. What say, Thierry? Shall we begin?" The Count removed the cap from the falcon's head, and she blinked in the sunlight, looking sharply left and right. He released her jesses and raised his arm. Settling her feathers, she flew with a shriek into the air.

Two days later, Isabelle sought out Father Benedict. She found the aged priest tending his vegetable garden, his sleeves rolled up above the elbows and the hem of his cassock tucked into his belt. He raised his arms in delight when he saw her, his cherubic face beaming. Wiping his hands and brow, he indicated a nearby bench, and they sat together beneath the shade of an apple tree.

"It has been a long time since last we spoke, my child. I have not seen you in the chapel as often as I would like."

"I apologize, Father. I have been remiss."

"I understand. I understand."

"Forgive my troubling you, but I wondered if I might discuss a small problem?"

"Mais bien sûr."

"I am at odds with my father. He hopes that I will accompany him to Paris for the royal festivities. I do not wish to hurt his feelings, yet I can barely manage my daily chores, let alone face so many people and pretend a liveliness I do not feel."

The old man leaned back on the bench, his legs stretched out in front of him. For a moment he seemed more interested in watching a bee that was searching for the last drop of nectar in a radiant yellow sunflower.

"Is the entire family planning to attend?" he asked finally.

"Yes. There will also be many friends, but that makes it more difficult. They will offer condolences, they will ask questions. So little time has passed since ... since ..." Her voice faded.

84

The priest nodded, and she looked away.

"I feel . . . Oh, it is difficult to speak of this. If I hold Aubrey's image—his memory—to myself, it seems to bind him to me, to keep him near in some way." A single tear rolled down her cheek.

"Ah, I see." Father Benedict reached up and plucked an apple from the tree. He rubbed it between his earth-stained hands, then polished it on the cloth of his robe and examined it carefully. He handed it to Isabelle and picked another for himself. Just as she concluded that their conversation must be over, he spoke once again.

"My daughter, I have seen much living and dying in the years I have been on this earth. When someone we love joins his Maker, we feel lonely and sad . . . though often I envy the one who makes that journey, for surely the kingdom that awaits him is glorious beyond all mea-sure. Your beloved was a beautiful young man of good character—a poet and a fair knight in every way. You feel, understandably, that he has seen God long before he should have . . . that he was taken from you too soon."

Isabelle's eyes were brimming with tears.

"We cannot know God's plan," the priest continued gently. "Only that there is one. Montdidier was called, and now he is at peace and in loving hands. It was his destiny. But it is not *your* destiny. You have an obligation to live the rest of the days that will be given you to the best of your ability . . . and the Lord will guide you, provided you do not waste or abuse this precious gift that is life."

Isabelle was now weeping openly, but for the first time since Montdidier's death, her tears were no longer of grief. She knelt and kissed Father Benedict's hand. Then, placing it against her cheek, she looked at him and nodded gratefully. He smiled and patted her shoulder, sensing that the worst was over.

Preparations began for the journey to Paris. DeNarsac saw to it that his men knew their assignments concerning the protection of the family. Carpenters checked their carts and wagons. Axles were greased, horses shod, harnesses renewed or polished. Oats and bales of hay were set aside for the journey.

Under the watchful eye of the steward, the officers of the household staff readied their departments. Rugs, sheepskins, and furs were aired, then beaten and stored in chests. Linens were washed and placed with bay leaves in crates made of cypress wood. The Count's wardrobe was packed, likewise his armor. Isabelle's gowns were folded carefully, her jewelry and toiletries stowed. Gifts were selected and wrapped. Pantry items, kitchen utensils, wines, candles, soaps, oils, and a selection of herbs from the garden—basil, chamomile, fennel, lavender, mint—all were itemized and readied for travel.

The Count was busy with Gilbert. The young man had been promoted from being DeNarsac's squire to his, and together they went over arrangements for the estate during the family's absence.

Thierry had so many chores, he ran back and forth endlessly. Though now officially DeNarsac's squire, he took it upon himself to ensure that Isabelle's needs were met. He also prepared Dragon for the trip, washing and grooming the hound until his lustrous white coat reflected the light. He noted that the dog's wounds had healed well, and that the scars were no longer visible beneath the regrowth of his fur. The boy packed his own wardrobe, which included new hose, a doublet, shoes, and a cloak that the Count had ordered for him.

The day of departure was clear and fresh. The church bell rang and villagers lined the route, waving farewell as the large convoy moved out from the château.

The Count of Montargis, Isabelle, and Thierry, each riding their own mount, were escorted by DeNarsac and his men-at-arms. Gilbert, the steward, and his staff followed, among them a butler, a pantler—to keep the pantry well stocked—two cooks, several valets, squires, and the family physician.

Painted wagons, with bright canopies of coarse wool, conveyed the ladies-in-waiting and other female staff. Carts, packhorses, and mules were weighed down with baggage. Grooms led extra horses for the long journey. Dragon and several guard dogs ran with the party.

Though it was late in the year to be traveling, the fine weather held. The roads were uneven and pitted, but they were able to accomplish approximately twenty-five miles each day. Progress was slower than when Thierry had traveled the same route with DeNarsac, just three Sabbaths ago, and the leisurely pace afforded the boy an opportunity to fully appreciate the late-autumn palette, which was still in full, riotous color. His thoughts turned to Montdidier, as they often did—and he reflected upon how the knight would have loved it.

Lodgings for the Count, his family, and the staff were

more than adequate, since the owners of the château at Moret-sur-Loing and the monks at the abbey of Vitry were used to accommodating visitors. They were amply rewarded for their hospitality with gifts and donations.

Béatrice, her husband, Alfonse, and their retinue joined the Montargis party at the abbey, and an evening of delicious food and spirited conversation was enjoyed by everyone. The following morning, the enlarged group of travelers moved on, arriving in Paris on the Monday evening.

Macaire sent word that he was delighted his family was in the city and was eager to see them. He would come as soon as his schedule allowed.

It took three long days to unpack, but finally all was accomplished, and the family settled comfortably into the Marais house.

On Friday, DeNarsac took advantage of a sunny autumn morning to spend an hour exercising Dragon. He and Thierry rode to the center of the city, the dog at their side. In this unfamiliar territory, DeNarsac had insisted Dragon wear a collar and leash for safety. The dog did not chafe at this restriction but padded contentedly beside his friends.

They tethered their horses and walked along the new moat of the King's fortress, the Louvre. White fluffy clouds moved across the skyline, nudged by a gentle breeze. Leaves spiraled from the trees, and there was a hint of wood smoke in the air. The elegant citizens of Paris were also appreciating the fine day. Nobles and dignitaries paraded in their finest silks and Flemish wools, and their colors complemented the season—reds, russets, ochers, violets. DeNarsac pointed out to Thierry the various berets that the merchants and craftsmen wore to represent membership in their respective guilds.

Thierry asked DeNarsac if he could walk Dragon, and the knight passed him the leash. The magnificent animal attracted much attention, and aware of the admiring glances, Thierry adopted a confident swagger, noted by DeNarsac with quiet amusement.

The knight recognized two ladies from the Court and stopped to greet them. They were charming, and effusive in their praise of Dragon.

"And who is this handsome young fellow?" one of them asked, glancing at Thierry.

"Such blue eyes! Such freckles!" said the other.

"*Mesdames,* I have the pleasure to introduce my new squire." DeNarsac placed a hand on Thierry's shoulder, and though the boy blushed, he felt a surge of pride in hearing himself so named. He observed the ladies' immaculate attire and thought them quite pretty . . . though not as lovely as Isabelle.

As DeNarsac continued to exchange pleasantries with them, Thierry's attention wandered to the fortress that would be the setting for the royal festivities on the morrow. The newly gilded turrets, shining in the sun, were reflected in the water of the moat. The boy tried to imagine what preparations were being made on the other side of the thick gray walls: what scurryings and polishings and setting of tables, what perfections were being asked of butlers and chefs and, in turn, their serving lads and scullery maids?

So lost was he in his reverie that it took a moment for him to recognize that something was wrong with Dragon. The fur on the back of the dog's neck was bristling and he was crouching low, his belly almost touching the ground. He emitted a guttural sound unlike any Thierry had heard before.

DeNarsac stopped his conversation and looked down in surprise. He glanced at Thierry, who shook his head in bewilderment.

"What is it, good fellow?" DeNarsac knelt beside the distressed animal. Dragon was growling, his upper lip curled. Grasping the leash a little tighter, Thierry scanned the crowd but saw nothing that could possibly have offended the dog. Surprisingly, however, he did see Isabelle in the distance, attended by her lady-in-waiting, and he called out to them.

Isabelle turned her head and acknowledged Thierry with a smile. With pleasure, he saw that Macaire was with her also, looking handsome and rakish in the livery of the King's Guard. He started toward them, but Dragon was already ahead of him, snarling and straining at the leash so hard that the boy almost lost his grip. He vaguely heard DeNarsac cry a warning as Dragon leaped for Macaire. Such was his strength that the knight would have been dashed to the ground had DeNarsac not rushed in to jerk the leash forcefully, pulling the dog clear.

Macaire staggered, and a murmur of concern came from people in the vicinity. They moved to a safer distance as Dragon continued to bark and growl.

DeNarsac grasped the dog firmly by the neck and collar.

"Hold, Dragon. HOLD!" he commanded fiercely.

The dog hesitated, bewildered. Then he obeyed.

"I am so sorry, Richard," DeNarsac gasped. "Milady, are you all right?"

"Yes . . . I . . ." Isabelle was pale and a little shaken. "*Hélas*, Dragon—what has come over you?" she said worriedly.

Whining, Dragon tried to shake free of DeNarsac's grip.

Macaire said, concerned, "Dragon. It is I, Macaire. You *know* me. . . ."

Thierry patted and stroked the dog, but Dragon would not be calmed. He was trembling, his body racked with shudders.

"He is not well." Thierry looked worriedly at DeNarsac.

"I fear that is so." The knight called to Macaire, "My deepest apologies, Richard. Please excuse us. We should return home." He took leave of the two ladies with whom he had been speaking, then said, "Come, Thierry, we must get the horses."

Macaire attempted to remove the dust that had marked his clothing.

"Richard, you are not hurt?" Isabelle was solicitous.

"Dear cousin, I am completely unharmed. But what a strange incident."

"Strange indeed. I pray the dog is not ill. He has been under stress these past months, yet he behaved as usual on the journey here. Perhaps the city is too stimulating for an animal so used to the country."

Macaire threw back his head and guffawed. "Oh, sweet Isabelle! If that were true, I would not wish to be present when Dragon had genuine cause for alarm. No malice intended, but it is more probable that living with DeNarsac has influenced the creature in some way."

"I don't understand. . . ." Isabelle was mystified. "Guy is but a gentle bear."

"You see that side of him, cousin, because you are kind and you seek the best in everyone. But he is also a great warrior, and warriors, of necessity, are brutal. You haven't seen Guy when he is among men . . . in a tavern, for example. You would not have been happy to witness his behavior as I did, a month ago. Our evening together ended in a dreadful *mêlée*. . . ."

Thierry and DeNarsac spoke little as they rode back from the city. DeNarsac was preoccupied, and Thierry saw him frown and glance often at the dog.

"What sickness could provoke him to behave like that?" Thierry finally asked. "He has never attacked anyone before. It is not in his nature."

DeNarsac frowned. "I have no answer," he replied. "Something may be revealed in the next few days."

The walk home calmed Dragon. He avoided eye contact with them, drank a great deal of water, and almost immediately lay down to sleep.

Watching him, Thierry said, "May I stay with him awhile?"

"Of course. I shall be within call if you need me."

Nestling beside Dragon, Thierry stroked him and put his lips to the dog's ear. "Please don't be ill, my friend. I couldn't bear to lose you, too."

Chapter Seven

THE FEAST

HE HERALDS STANDING ON either side of *Le Grand Vis*—the magnificent staircase in the Louvre—raised their trumpets and sounded a fanfare.

The guests began moving toward the banquet hall, and Thierry, following the Count and Isabelle up the stairs, was charged with expectation and excitement. Though he had experienced a life of privilege, nothing had prepared him for the grandeur of the palace and the style of the people present, all of whom were dressed in their finest brocades, velvets, silks, satins, and jewels.

As they entered the great hall, Thierry drew in his breath with amazement. The theme for the Feast of Saint Martin was a simple one—that of the countryside—and the room had been decorated much like a garden. But the extraordinary part was that the trees and foliage, the flowers and fruit, had all been painted with gold. Glowing lanterns hung from the branches, torches flared in sconces on the walls, two huge chandeliers in the ceiling were ablaze with candles. There was a platform at the far end of the hall, surmounted by a canopy of gold with a magnificent throne beneath. Tables with benches flanked each side of the room and were set with silver and gold plate, beakers and footed goblets, delicately wrought finger bowls, and garlands of flowers. The centerpiece on each was a gilded swan swimming on a lake of polished silver. In the minstrels' gallery, musicians played soothing and elegant music on lutes, reeds, and harp.

Thierry was seated at a table with his family, Béatrice, Alfonse, and DeNarsac. As soon as the guests were assembled, trumpets rang out again and everyone stood as His Majesty, King Charles V, entered, surrounded by his courtiers.

He wore a blue velvet robe embroidered with gold *fleurs-de-lis*. A cape of ermine was around his shoulders, a gold crown upon his head. He looked small and incredibly frail.

DeNarsac informed Thierry, "The man nearest the

King is the Royal Chamberlain, Bureau de la Rivière. The three men following with their wives are the King's brothers, the Dukes of Anjou, Berry, and Burgundy. They are known as the Princes of the *Fleur-de-Lis*. You recognize Bertrand Du Guesclin, I am sure. The last gentleman is Thomas de Pizan, the King's astrologer."

"And there is Macaire!" Thierry pointed. The Knight was standing near the King, and he smiled and nodded as Thierry waved at him.

The boy whispered, "Why is Her Majesty, the Queen, not present?"

"They say she is fragile and does not attend many appointments these days."

"The King looks to be the fragile one," Thierry remarked. "He is so gaunt and pale."

"With good reason," DeNarsac declared. "He has many ailments, sustained since childhood. His father was captured by the British and imprisoned. He lost two daughters to the Black Death and several other children in infancy. He wrestles with the war against the English on a daily basis, not to mention his problems with the Pope. . . ."

"Why does he wear furs and silver-cuffed gloves?" Thierry asked.

"It is said he feels the cold," DeNarsac replied. "The gloves, I think, divert attention from a fistulous wound on his left arm. It was created by his physician to drain the humors from his system, and he must keep it open for his continued health."

Thierry stared at the King and wondered how such a sickly man could find the stamina to rule an entire realm.

The Royal Chamberlain held up a hand for silence. He welcomed the guests, then requested that all remain standing while the Bishop of Paris recited the blessing. That done, the musicians began to play once again, and bearers brought in ewers of water, pouring it into the silver bowls so that the guests might wash their hands.

Isabelle touched Thierry on the shoulder.

"Be careful how much you eat when the first course is served, for there will be at least five courses to follow and many, many choices. Also, be mindful not to slurp or belch or blow on your food."

Thierry smiled at her. She was looking radiant, wearing a silk peach-colored gown, belted low over the hips, and elegant pointed shoes. A white cape was caught at each shoulder by a rose-colored clasp, and her fair hair was coiffed in a mist of jewels.

Butlers and their staff carried in tureens and platters of food. There were three choices of soup—a cinnamon broth, a green soup of eels, and a marrowbone *consommé*. There were capon pies, meat pies, roasted partridges and plovers. For members of the clergy, who seldom ate meat, there was roast bream, turbot, and sole, and a black oyster stew. There were white beets and peas, beans and turnips, and an accompaniment of sauces and wines.

Thierry helped serve Isabelle and the Count, then took for himself a small portion of a meat pie with some vegetables. He noted that Alfonse seemed particularly fond of the oyster stew. He glanced toward the King's table and saw the royal family being served with their own covered dishes and a taster sampling every item placed before His Majesty. He asked DeNarsac about it, and the knight shrugged.

"One must always ensure the safety of the King."

Thierry thought it must be exhausting to be cosseted in such a manner every moment of one's life.

The first course concluded, the platters, trenchers, and tureens were cleared. Jugglers and acrobats ran into the room and performed amazing acts of contortion and daring. Guests rose to stretch their legs and to socialize, Béatrice being among the first to seize the opportunity to mingle with the members of parliament, ambassadors, diverse lords, and foreign dignitaries. There was a great deal of merriment and noise.

The second course was more exotic than the first. This was presented by Knights of the Court, who considered it an honor to offer their services in deference to their King. They made a spectacular entrance, each carrying a silver tray with a roasted goose upon it, the traditional dish of Martinmas. Thierry was reminded of the legend of his favorite saint, Martin of Tours, an eccentric soldier turned monk, whose hiding place was revealed by the raucous bird.

Thierry tried to count how many geese had been purchased for the royal feast, but abandoned the attempt when he saw all the other dishes being served: roasted venison and frumenty, little pancakes, larks and turtle-doves in pastry, crayfish and perch. Alfonse requested a double helping of hot sauce with his generous portion of boar's tails.

Macaire came down from the high table to visit.

Béatrice held out her arms to him, and he embraced her, kissing her on both cheeks. Alfonse raised a goblet in salute to his son.

Macaire said, "I have a surprise for you, Thierry. His Majesty has asked to speak with the Count, and I have arranged for you and Isabelle to be presented."

Thierry gasped.

"And what about me?" Béatrice demanded.

"You, too, Mother."

"How did you manage that?" Thierry asked.

Macaire winked. "His Majesty admires my blue eyes."

DeNarsac said, "Richard, I hope you are none the worse for yesterday's encounter with Dragon?"

"I haven't given it another thought," Macaire replied. "I was only worried that it might spoil the few precious moments I was able to spend with Isabelle."

She blushed. "Cousin, you are generous to consider us when you are on duty and so busy."

Macaire gave a mock bow. "What is family for?" He kissed Isabelle's hand. "I shall return for you all shortly."

The second course was cleared away, and to Thierry's delight a troupe of performing dogs and monkeys was led into the hall and began executing clever tricks.

The extraordinary feast continued. Thierry began to feel that he could not eat another morsel. Yet when he saw the sugared, fried bread slices and the cream fritters, he could not resist taking a portion of each, though he paled at the shad pies, jellied eels and lampreys, roast pigs, bacon gruel, and Spanish crackling that were also offered.

A company of actors entered. In keeping with the pastoral theme of the gala, they were dressed as country characters—the hay maker, the farmer, the sheepherder, the plowman, the latter guiding a fake horse with two actors inside. All the roles were performed by men, even the milking maids, the farmer's wife, the goose girl. It was rollicking, silly entertainment, and the guests had eaten and drunk enough to be thoroughly amused by it. The troupe exited to much applause and had to be brought back for a second bow. Alfonse fell asleep.

Macaire returned and said, "It is time." He glanced at his father.

"Leave him," said Béatrice. "He'll only make a fool of himself, and embarrass us all."

They made their way to the royal table. Béatrice

announced grandly so that all could hear, "How pleasant to see His Majesty again! We were hunting together just three months ago at Vincennes."

The Count placed his arm lightly about Thierry's shoulder.

"When you first meet His Majesty, do not speak until you are spoken to."

"Yes, sir."

"Stand tall, and answer courteously and truthfully."

"I will, sir."

Béatrice paused to greet Du Guesclin.

"*Connétable!* What a pleasure to see you again!"

He rose hurriedly from his chair, dabbing his mouth with a kerchief. "Madame! I trust you are well?"

Macaire bowed before the Royal Chamberlain and said, "I have the Count of Montargis and his family at the request of His Majesty."

"Ah, yes." The Chamberlain nodded and encouraged them to step forward as Macaire turned back to release Du Guesclin from his mother's fawning attention.

The King greeted the Count.

"Gilles! It has been many months since we were in Montargis."

"Your Majesty." The Count knelt before him in obeisance.

"Rise, good fellow. We wished to mention that we will be paying you another visit sometime in the spring."

"Sire, we will be greatly honored."

"Now that Vincennes is complete, and the library here does not need as much attention, I have been thinking about enlarging the château—making it more habitable. When last I visited you, I felt I was still living in the thirteenth century."

"Your taste is always impeccable, Majesty."

"*Chère* Isabelle, you are the prettiest lady in the room." Isabelle curtsied as the King turned to her. "We were deeply saddened to hear of your loss, my dear. Aubrey de Montdidier was one of our finest, and we miss him very much."

Thierry was standing a few paces away. Now that he could study the King close at hand, he felt a sense of awe, for in spite of his fragility the monarch had an air of intelligence, composure, and nobility that commanded respect. He had a generous mouth, a high forehead, and an aristocratic nose.

"And may I present my ward, Thierry?" the Count

was saying. Thierry started and moved forward to bow. He discovered that he was trembling. Looking up at the King, he noticed that he was wearing several gold chains about his neck from which dangled little bottles and amulets.

"Young man, you have been the subject of some discussion lately," the King said. Thierry's eyes widened. "Are you the owner of the white wolfhound?"

"Oh—well, not exactly, Sire. . . ." Thierry stumbled over his words. "As you may know, Dragon belonged to Aubrey de Montdidier. We—we all love him, but in truth he is now the property of Guy, Sieur DeNarsac, Captain of the Count's men-at-arms."

"Is he with us this evening?"

"Yes, Sire. He is there." Thierry pointed.

"We would be interested to meet him." The King gestured to his Chamberlain, who immediately dispatched a courtier to fetch DeNarsac.

"You will not remember, Thierry, but I knew you when you were a very small boy. I was not King at the time, but the Regent. You were perhaps three—the age of my eldest son now." The King turned to the Count. "Time has wings, Gilles. Your boy will soon be a man."

"Yes, Your Majesty."

"Do you read, Thierry?" the King inquired.

"Yes, Sire."

"Do you study Latin?"

"Yes, Sire."

"Then you are intelligent as well as handsome. *Legendo discimus.*"

Thierry tipped his head in thought, then translated, "By reading we learn?"

"*Bravo!* Would you care to visit my library one day? I have just commissioned some splendid new volumes."

"I should like that very much, Sire!"

"I shall arrange it."

"Thank you, Your Majesty."

DeNarsac arrived and Thierry, the Count, and Isabelle stepped aside as he was presented. The King scrutinized the knight.

"You are the man who recovered the body of our good friend Montdidier?"

"Yes, Your Majesty." DeNarsac bowed.

"Is it true that his wolfhound was responsible for leading you and the boy to the grave?"

"Completely true, Sire."

"That is remarkable. He must be a unique creature."

"Dragon is a noble animal in every way, Your Majesty."

"We would like to see this Dragon for ourselves. You may bring him to Court tomorrow. Shall we say midday?"

"It will be my pleasure, Sire."

"Has there been progress in determining who killed Montdidier?"

"Alas no, Sire. It is still a mystery."

". . . And a tragedy for all concerned," the King concurred.

"May I take this opportunity to congratulate Your Majesty on your choice of Richard Macaire as Montdidier's successor. He must be an extremely capable leader of the Royal Bodyguard."

The King chuckled.

"Hardly *my* choice, dear fellow. I have never witnessed such a blatant push for promotion. But he *is* the correct person for the job. Ah, Béatrice! Dear lady, how enchanting you look this evening!"

Béatrice had thrust herself in front of DeNarsac, and she curtsied to the floor.

Behind her, Macaire gave DeNarsac a look of apology. DeNarsac held up his hand, indicating he took no offense. He returned to his table, where sweetmeats and fruit had been served—pomegranates, roasted figs, pears and apples, almonds, candied orange peel and ginger, all with an accompaniment of sweet wines and exquisite hand-carved sugar sculptures.

"*Mon Dieu*, Guy!" Thierry babbled excitedly. "What a thrill! What a day this has been! His Majesty invited me to see his library!"

"But that is wonderful!" DeNarsac smiled at his enthusiasm.

"You know, I was wrong, Guy. I thought at first that he looked—odd, somehow, not like a King should look. But he has an inner strength—and knowledge. . . ."

DeNarsac nodded. "That is why he is called Charles the Wise."

The minstrels in the gallery began to play a slow and stately theme.

"So, Thierry, you learned something today. Judge not according to the appearance. A book may not be determined by its binding."

"As His Majesty would be the first to say!" Thierry agreed. He followed DeNarsac's gaze and saw that he was watching Macaire dancing with Isabelle. For the first time in months, she looked happy, and as Macaire whispered something to her, she threw back her head, laughing.

Thierry was delighted. He glanced back at DeNarsac, wishing to share the moment, but he said nothing . . . for the knight's face betrayed an emotion that Thierry felt embarrassed to witness. With a catch in his heart, he suddenly knew that DeNarsac yearned to be the one making Isabelle laugh, and that he, too, adored her with every fiber of his being.

Chapter Eight
THE STORM

eNARSAC AND THIERRY DEPARTED for the Louvre with Dragon early the following morning. Rain clouds formed a low ceiling over the city, and a fine drizzle had set in. They wanted to leave time to prepare Dragon for his royal visit, as his white coat would be muddied from the walk and in need of attention.

Upon arrival, they presented their names to a sentry and were escorted to a courtyard by the palace stables. As a groom led away their horses, they glimpsed the Royal Chamberlain scurrying across the quadrangle. He was clutching files and papers to his chest in an attempt to keep them dry, but at sight of them he changed course to greet them.

"Ah, the famous canine." He smiled, extending a

hand to Dragon. The dog touched it with his nose, then pushed his head into the Chamberlain's palm and wagged his tail in greeting. "What a splendid fellow! His Majesty will be delighted to make his acquaintance."

DeNarsac said, "Permit us to express our gratitude concerning yesterday—it was an event we will long remember."

"We are lucky the rain held off until today." The Chamberlain patted Dragon. "I fear we are in for a spell. When does the Count depart for Montargis?"

"We hope to leave the day after tomorrow, sir. Weather permitting."

"Well, we must trust that it clears for you. Now let me take you to a room where you can remain dry until your appointment with His Majesty."

There was a commotion behind them, and a horse-drawn wagon entered the yard.

"Am I expected to wade through this mud, or is someone willing to offer an alternative?" said a familiar voice.

It was Béatrice.

Lieutenant Landry hurried from the stables looking flustered and ran to fetch the wooden steps that would enable her to dismount.

"Remain calm, Mother! I am here, and I shall carry you, if need be." Macaire appeared at the door, smiling as he strode toward the wagon.

Neither Thierry nor DeNarsac had a chance to prevent what happened next. Dragon became a blur of white as he launched himself upon Macaire. The force of his assault dashed the knight to the ground, and he became spattered with mud as he landed in a puddle. Had he not brought up his arm to protect his throat, the dog would surely have gone for his jugular.

DeNarsac and Lieutenant Landry rushed in to haul the snarling animal away. A groom ran over to help. Béatrice screamed hysterically, and the Chamberlain moved to comfort her. Men of the King's Guard came out to see what the commotion was about. Thierry remained rooted to the spot, stunned that Dragon had committed another transgression.

The dog continued to growl and bark, and would have lunged again but for DeNarsac's firm hold on him. The knight shook him, reprimanding him severely.

"For *shame*, Dragon! What is this behavior? NO, Dragon! Desist, you *bad* fellow!"

Macaire got to his feet. He was shaken and embarrassed, and vented his nervous rage.

"*Nom d'un nom*, Guy! What do you think you are doing? The dog has become a savage lunatic! He should not be allowed to roam the city. Have you no *sense*?"

"Richard, I—I do not know what to say . . ." DeNarsac stammered. "You know Dragon as well as I—"

Béatrice hiked up her skirts and waded through the mud. Oblivious to Dragon's proximity, she whacked DeNarsac on the shoulder.

"How dare you provoke these attacks on my son? Can you not keep the brute contained? *Mon Dieu!* He should be destroyed—he is a danger to the public!"

"Mother, please—keep away from the dog," Macaire begged her.

She turned to the Chamberlain.

"I am glad you are a witness here, my dear Bureau. It is not the first time this has happened, you know."

"Madame, this is truly unfortunate. May I suggest you go inside and take a glass of something warm? You should not be standing here in the rain." The Chamberlain looked at DeNarsac. "Under the circumstances you cannot bring the dog before His Majesty. I will make your excuses."

"I hope you will fully inform him of this incident," Béatrice prattled on. "In fact, I would prefer to see His Majesty myself if he is free—"

"Mother, that is *not* necessary," Macaire said sharply.

She swayed and took his arm.

"*Mon cher*, take me to your chambers. I am so undone, I may faint."

As they departed, Macaire called over his shoulder to DeNarsac, "We will discuss this! Meanwhile, I suggest you keep that beast locked up where he can do no further harm."

The Chamberlain said, "Excuse me now. His Majesty will be wondering where I am. We have a full day ahead of us." He hurried across the courtyard, leaving DeNarsac and Thierry standing in the rain with the sodden Dragon beside them.

They returned to the Marais. Thierry felt miserable. The morning's incident had been dreadful, and he knew that consequences would surely follow. But beneath his concern there was an underlying fear—something just out of reach: a sense of evil and danger. He could not grasp what it meant, but it evoked long-buried feelings. Much as he tried to push them away, they kept nudging the edge of his consciousness.

The knight wearily sank into a chair in his quarters and watched as Thierry kindled a fire so that they might all become warm and dry. The boy fetched a cloth and began to towel Dragon. The only sounds in the room were the crackle and spit of the flames and the rain pattering lightly on the roof.

After a moment, Thierry said quietly, "Guy, I have a question."

DeNarsac looked up, and the boy continued.

"Why Macaire? What is it about him that makes Dragon behave in this manner?"

The knight gazed into the fire, a troubled look on his face.

Thierry continued. "He used to be friendly with Macaire, so what has changed?"

"There are many possibilities." DeNarsac rubbed a hand across his eyes. "We may be seeing the onset of some disease, as we suspected earlier."

"But then wouldn't Dragon assail everyone?" Thierry pressed. "Why only Macaire?"

"Perhaps there is something about Macaire's appearance. For example, Dragon has never seen him in livery before. Dogs have been known to dislike people in dark clothing."

"But Macaire often wears dark clothing," Thierry countered.

"Then the only other explanation is that something happened between them. Something we know nothing of. . . ."

Thierry stared at the dog thoughtfully. What could have occurred between Dragon and Macaire? And when?

DeNarsac said, "Just as before, Dragon will not look at me. I fear he is very unhappy."

Thierry hesitated, then said gently, "I think you made his heart heavy today."

DeNarsac looked surprised. "I would think, if anything, he senses my disappointment in him."

"Perhaps that, too. But you berated him, and I believe he feels it keenly."

"What could I do?" DeNarsac suddenly burst out. "I had to make him take heed—for his own sake. Oh,

Dragon." He extended his arm. "Forgive me, good friend. I would never knowingly cause you grief."

The dog whined and crept to him, placing his head on the knight's outstretched palm.

The dinner hour came and passed.

Neither man felt like company, and Thierry fetched a simple meal of bread and cheese and ale and brought Dragon his platter of food. The dog turned his head away when it was offered to him, and would not eat.

"You see, he *is* unwell," Thierry said, worried.

They were startled by a loud knock on the door. A young messenger from the Court stood outside. He handed Thierry a letter. "From the Royal Chamberlain, for Sieur DeNarsac," he explained.

DeNarsac came to the door. "You are soaked, boy. Would you care to come in and get dry?"

The messenger shook his head. "Thank you, sir, but I must return. I am expected back at Court." He hurried away.

A flurry of wet leaves blew in through the door, and Thierry hastily shut it. He waited anxiously while the knight read the contents of the letter.

"His Majesty wishes to speak with us tomorrow on matters concerning Dragon. It seems Lady Béatrice has lodged a formal complaint, and Dragon's fate now lies in the royal hands."

Thierry drew in his breath. "What time tomorrow?"

"We must be at the palace by nine in the morning."

DeNarsac crossed to Dragon and knelt beside him, cupping a hand beneath his chin.

"If you could only speak to us—tell us what troubles you," he said wistfully. "Would Montdidier have understood, I wonder?" He rubbed the dog's ears and touched his nose. It was cold. "What say, old fellow, how about eating a morsel, hmm?"

But once again Dragon refused. With a deep sigh he lay down, his head on his paws, his dark eyes unblinking as he gazed at his master.

Something about the dog's pose struck a chord with the knight, and he struggled to place it.

Thierry said, "I will bring my pallet near the fire and be with him."

"Good. Try to let the events of the day pass from your

119

mind. Worrying tonight will not solve anything." DeNarsac went into his bedchamber and shut the thick wooden door.

Thierry stoked the fire and put out the lamp. He settled next to Dragon and laid his head on the dog's strong back. Dragon's damp fur had a pleasant, musky odor. The embers created a smoky haze, and the sound of the rain outside calmed the boy's troubled thoughts. He drifted into sleep.

An hour later, lightning split open the sky and thunder erupted overhead.

Thierry sat up, and Dragon emitted a low warning growl.

Thierry patted him. "It's all right, boy, it is only the storm."

There was another flash, and DeNarsac also woke, then settled himself more comfortably.

A cannon of thunder boomed, and just after it came another sound—the smallest thud. DeNarsac stiffened, not sure what he had heard, or even if he had heard anything. But then came a whisper of cloth.

Someone else was in the room.

Carefully, slowly, the knight slid his hand beneath his pillow, his fingers encircling his dagger. Flashes of lightning came rapidly. Glancing to a small mirror across from him, DeNarsac briefly saw a silhouette against the window.

The shadowy figure stood a moment, still as a statue, then advanced stealthily to the bed.

There was the gleam of a knife in his hand. Swiftly he brought it up to strike, but DeNarsac was quicker, blocking the dagger in a jarring defense with his own blade.

In one smooth movement, he threw the coverlet aside, rolled to his feet, and unsheathed his sword from its resting place by the bedpost. The would-be assassin drew his own sword, and in the shadows, the two men circled each other warily, seeking the moment to take advantage.

DeNarsac heard his opponent's labored breathing and smelled the odor of alcohol on his breath. Another flash of light, and DeNarsac made his move, attempting a head cut. It was clumsily blocked, and the knight gauged that though his attacker had strength, he had little talent.

Steel met steel as the fight ensued. With only intermittent light to guide him, DeNarsac relied on his instincts, thrusting and ducking, twisting and lunging, whirling, darting, gradually forcing his masked opponent into a corner.

With a circular sweep of his sword, he disarmed him and touched the tip of his blade to the man's throat.

"Who are you?" he growled.

There was a movement behind him. DeNarsac spun around to discover a second intruder just inches away.

Sidestepping and parrying the swift blow that would have sliced through his ribs, he knew instantly that this new adversary was more dangerous; there was definite skill in his swordplay.

As DeNarsac endured another onslaught, the first man swept up his fallen sword and joined the fray. With two men attacking him, the knight was hard-pressed, and it took every trick he knew, every ounce of concentration, to keep them at bay.

The second attacker panted, "I can take him now. Check the dog."

"He is not here," the first man growled, his voice rough and coarse.

"Try the other room." The second attacker swung viciously, and DeNarsac ducked as the blade whistled above him, missing his head by a fraction.

The first assassin ran for the heavy door and grasped the handle, pulling it toward him.

Dragon exploded into the chamber, hurling himself upon DeNarsac's aggressor. He sank his teeth into his sword arm. The man howled with pain and fell to the floor, dropping his weapon.

Thierry rushed in, brandishing a fire iron.

"Thierry, be careful!" DeNarsac yelled, but it was too late.

The first intruder came from behind the door and grasped the boy in his arms. Thierry struggled bravely, swinging, kicking, biting. The man grabbed a fistful of his hair, jerked his head backward, and pressed cold steel to his throat.

Thierry froze. DeNarsac froze. The fire iron clattered to the floor.

DeNarsac said sharply, "Do not be hasty. Harm the boy and your guts will spill before you can blink."

"Call off the dog," demanded the man, and he applied more pressure to the knife.

The wounded attacker was clutching his arm, rolling in agony, Dragon's teeth mere inches from his face.

The man said again, "Call him off, I say, or the boy is finished."

"Hold, Dragon. HOLD!" DeNarsac commanded.

Dragon obeyed, trembling.

"Good Dragon. Enough." DeNarsac placed one hand on the dog's neck, the other still holding his sword at the ready.

The injured intruder scrambled to his feet, cursing as he stumbled for the window. Tumbling over the wide sill, he fled into the dark, wet night. The man holding Thierry flung the boy to the floor, raced into the other room, and tore open the front door. He fled down the gallery and vanished.

DeNarsac rushed to Thierry's side.

"Are you all right, boy?"

Thierry rose shakily to his feet, dazed and winded.

"Yes, sir. You?"

"I am unharmed."

DeNarsac ran to the door and looked outside.

"*Par le ciel!* I wish I could have seen who they were." He shut the door firmly behind him, throwing the bolt. Lighting a lantern, he quickly and thoroughly checked both rooms and pulled shut the bedroom window.

Picking up the assailant's sword from the floor, he examined it, turning it over in his hands.

"I don't recognize it," he said. "But it bears the maker's seal. And an encircled *S*. That tells us something."

"What does it tell us?" Thierry asked in a shaky voice.

"The encircled *S* stands for the Latin *'O Sancta . . .'*"

"'O Blessed . . .'" Thierry translated.

"Indeed. So we may surmise that our man is reasonably well born, probably educated. He certainly fought with skill."

He poured two beakers of wine and handed one to the boy.

"Let us rekindle the fire. We still stay together tonight . . . what is left of it. We must be vigilant from now on, for whoever they were, they did not get what they wanted."

"Guy, why would anyone wish to harm you?" Thierry threw more logs on the fire.

DeNarsac sank into his chair and sipped from his cup. Exhausted, he laid his head against the dark leather, his eyes closed. He did not offer an answer.

Thierry sat at his feet, his knees under his chin. He

was trembling, his heart still pounding. Dragon came to lie beside them.

"Dragon was brave—a formidable adversary." Thierry stroked the dog.

"Indeed, I would wish him at my side in battle any day," DeNarsac murmured, patting the boy's shoulder.

Thierry's mind raced, his thoughts spinning to recall faces, names, anyone they had encountered in Paris who might bear a grudge or have reason to harm DeNarsac. Surely no one would hold the knight responsible for Dragon's recent behavior?

"Guy . . . anyone who knows you would know Dragon would protect you," Thierry reasoned. "Does that mean that the men tonight were strangers?"

DeNarsac sat up. "*Non, par Dieu!* He said, 'Check the dog.' I almost recognized his voice."

"What do you mean?" Thierry asked.

"I mean before you came in, Thierry, the man distinctly said, 'Check the dog.' He knew of Dragon . . . it was almost as if he expected something." His eyes searched the room. "What would he wish to check? *Why?*" His glance took in the dog's platter of food. With an exclamation, he rose and strode to pick it up. Revealed in the shadows beside it, a rat lay writhing on the floor—quivering in the last agonies of a terrible death.

"Here is our answer, Thierry," DeNarsac said grimly. "They were not strangers. They must have assumed Dragon had eaten and that he was dead, so they felt it safe to go after me. Thank the Lord he would not touch the food. This rat was not so fortunate."

As comprehension dawned in the boy's eyes, the knight flung the plate and its contents into the fire.

Chapter Nine

THE ACCUSATION

HIERRY WAS UNABLE TO sleep. He had been truly terrified, the old nightmares threatening to return. He thought again of his parents, who had been murdered so long ago. Had their assassins used the cover of darkness to kill them as those last night had so nearly killed DeNarsac? And how had Dragon's meat been poisoned? He himself had collected it from the table scraps that were always set aside for the dog.

The storm had blown itself out by morning.

Thierry and DeNarsac were at the stables early. The air was raw and cold, and Paris was still dripping with moisture.

Noticing the boy's pale, worried face, DeNarsac said, "I do not want you out of my sight. I am not sure who can be trusted at the moment."

"What shall we do with Dragon while we are at the Louvre?"

"He, too, must not be left alone. Gilbert will take care of him. He is one person we *can* trust."

Thierry asked another question that had been haunting him.

"Guy, why would someone try to kill Dragon?"

DeNarsac said grimly, "I cannot answer yet, Thierry. Careful, here comes Lady Isabelle. She should not be told about the intruders—certainly not before our audience with the King."

Isabelle was hurrying across the courtyard.

"Oh, Guy, I wanted a word with you. I understand you are to see His Majesty this morning. Béatrice informed us of Dragon's second attack on Macaire. It is dreadful. I wonder you didn't tell me about it. . . . I suspect you have been avoiding me."

DeNarsac looked uncomfortable. "Milady—we returned late, the rain was so heavy. . . . But yes, in truth, I did not wish to worry you."

"Guy, I am not a child. You do not have to shield me from life as you used to. I am keen to know all that happens in our little family—especially where Thierry is concerned."

There was a coolness to her demeanor that startled Thierry. It was so uncharacteristic of Isabelle. He glanced at DeNarsac and saw a look of bewilderment on his face.

But the knight replied courteously. "I accept your instruction, Milady, and will try to be more considerate."

Isabelle looked at Dragon, and the dog wagged his tail halfheartedly. She patted his head and looked up as if about to say something else, but then thought better of it and walked away.

They left Dragon in Gilbert's safe care and, before departing, went briefly to see the Count. He was in an irritable mood, and he berated DeNarsac and Thierry for not being more responsible with the dog—but he became instantly attentive, then concerned, when DeNarsac related the events of the previous evening.

"*Grace à Dieu* neither of you was harmed," he said gravely. "We will discuss this further after you have seen His Majesty. Report to me the instant you return. Meanwhile, be careful. And see that Dragon is well protected."

✦ ✦ ✦

Bureau de la Rivière was waiting for them as they arrived at Court.

"Follow me, please," he said crisply, and led them along a glass-domed gallery to a small antechamber. "His Majesty is waiting for you."

A large clock on the mantelpiece was striking the hour as they were ushered into the royal presence.

King Charles was seated in a high-backed chair behind a magnificent desk. Thierry noted again how thin and frail he looked.

The monarch wasted no time getting to the point.

"Sieur DeNarsac, I have had an earful about you from Lady Béatrice, and I have also spoken with the Chevalier Macaire. To his credit, he is loath to press charges, but *she* is insistent. I would like to hear your version of these attacks by the dog."

Thierry looked at DeNarsac. The knight hesitated.

The King said testily, "Come now. The animal is dangerous, and something must be done about him. The only reason I have held my judgment thus far is that he has acquired a certain *mystique* since the discovery of Aubrey de Montdidier."

DeNarsac said, "Your Majesty, I wonder if I might

speak with you privately?" He glanced toward Bureau de la Rivière, who was standing behind the King.

"Anything you have to say can be said with Bureau present. Please do as I ask."

Haltingly, DeNarsac spoke about the two incidents concerning Macaire and Dragon. He described clearly and simply how, twice, Dragon had launched himself upon Macaire, having never before attacked anyone.

"His behavior has always been exemplary, Your Majesty," he concluded. "I would swear on my life that these episodes can be justified in some way, and that the dog is harmless."

The monarch glanced at Thierry. "Anything to add, young man?" he asked.

Thierry thought a moment, then said, "No, Sire. Sieur DeNarsac has spoken truthfully. That is exactly what happened, and I feel as he does."

The King was quiet, playing absently with the chains and amulets around his neck. He turned to his Chamberlain.

"What say, Bureau? You've heard both sides. . . . The others say the dog is a vicious brute, a menace."

"Your Majesty, I personally saw the dog yesterday morning. Though we had never met, I confess his demeanor toward me was friendly and gentle. It was only when the Chevalier Macaire appeared that he changed."

"Well, exemplary or not, the dog is now a problem. We cannot let him simply roam among the populace. This viciousness may be latent, and who knows whom he might assault next? So . . . what is to be done?" He tapped his fingers on the desk and fixed DeNarsac with a piercing gaze. "Perhaps the dog has *la rage*—the mad disease?"

"I would swear not, Your Majesty . . . for he would not solely go after Macaire."

"Quite so." The King nodded. "You are *sure* that Macaire is the only person the dog has attacked thus far?"

DeNarsac drew in his breath and hesitated once more. "Your Majesty. There was an incident last night . . ."

"Aha! So there *is* more. I thought as much. There is *always* more."

Thierry's stomach was churning with anxiety. He wanted the King to know what had happened, but if they told him about Dragon's attack upon the intruder, would His Majesty understand that, this time, the dog had been trying to protect them?

"Speak up, speak up." The King sounded impatient.

"We—we had retired last evening, Sire. There was an intruder. I challenged him. There was a fight. A second intruder appeared. Dragon and Thierry were in the next room and came to my aid. Dragon did attack one of the men, but only in my defense. His strength was such that neither could finish what they intended, and they fled."

The King's mouth was open with amazement. He managed to say, "And what was it they intended?"

DeNarsac replied quietly, "It seems they wished to kill me, your Majesty. I believe they thought Dragon was already dead, for his food had been poisoned. They would not have been so foolish as to attempt an assassination if the dog were still alive. Mercifully, Dragon had not eaten."

The King looked at Bureau de la Rivière, then back at DeNarsac. Finally his gaze settled on Thierry.

"Young fellow—tell this to me again, in *your* words. Every detail."

His heart thumping, Thierry described his part in the previous night's drama: how he and Dragon had been asleep, how the storm had awakened them, and that it was Dragon who knew that something was wrong in

DeNarsac's chamber and had alerted him to go and check.

The King said to the knight, "Do you know why someone would wish you—and the dog—dead?"

A look of grief crossed DeNarsac's face, and he lifted his head and gazed at a spot on the ceiling. After a second, he replied, "Your Majesty, I fear the incidents we are speaking about are not random acts, but part of a greater whole. What I am compelled to say comes strictly from my knowledge of Dragon—my love for him, to be sure, but also my trust and faith in him." He paused, gasping as if he could not draw breath.

"Go on," the King encouraged him, his face solemn.

"I believe—I *feel*—that Dragon is trying to tell us something. I sense these attacks on Macaire are not capricious, not mere viciousness, but an attempt to right some wrong. I . . . it's about Montdidier, you see. Dear God, what am I saying?" His hand touched his brow.

"If I understand correctly, you are suggesting that Macaire played some part in Montdidier's death. And the dog was a witness and is attempting to convey that to us?"

"Yes, Sire."

"That seems rather far-fetched."

"I agree, Your Majesty. Yet my intuition tells me it is so. Whatever the case, someone wishes Dragon dead."

"And you also," the King stated quietly.

"I . . . don't know."

Thierry had been aghast during the exchange, and now he cried aloud.

The King looked at him sharply.

"You seem surprised, Thierry."

"It's just that . . ." Thierry stared at DeNarsac. "You never spoke of this before. You never told me you were thinking this way."

"Thierry, until last night it was too painful to contemplate."

The King said, "*Alors*, these are serious accusations. It would be too much to hope that you have proof of some kind?"

"Sire, I have none. A sword was dropped by one of the intruders last night. It bears the maker's seal, but I cannot tell to whom it belongs. The only thing I *am* sure of is Dragon: his nature, his character. He has never before attacked anyone. He is a gentle, noble animal. He was Montdidier's animal. . . ." DeNarsac's voice was charged with emotion.

King Charles inhaled deeply, straightening his back as he placed both hands on his desk.

"Here is what we will do." He stood up. "We will see the dog for ourselves. Let a King look at this creature and determine whether he is a docile hound or a fire-breathing dragon."

Bureau de la Rivière said, "Your Majesty, are you sure that is wise—considering his recent behavior?"

"Dear fellow, I have spent a lifetime avoiding dangers greater than most people could imagine. Besides, if the animal is as honorable as you all claim, then I have nothing to fear." He looked at DeNarsac. "God help you if your assumptions are wrong. You must know that there are rumors about you, too; that some say *you* are inciting the dog's behavior." The King sighed. "The Court is a hive of intrigue, which I navigate daily. Therefore . . . you, DeNarsac, will remain here. Thierry will fetch the dog, and we shall meet again this afternoon. Bureau, summon Thomas de Pizan. I have need of his celestial counsel."

DeNarsac and Thierry bowed as the King prepared to leave. He paused at the door.

"One more thing. Do not give the dog nourishment until after our appointment." He swept out of the room.

The Chamberlain was saying to DeNarsac, "If you would come with me, please ..."

DeNarsac said hurriedly, "Thierry, when you bring Dragon, ask Gilbert to accompany you. You and Dragon must not be alone. Be very alert, very careful."

Thierry nodded. "I will return as soon as possible. Should I inform Isabelle?"

"By all means."

"Everything?"

"Yes." The knight gave Thierry a reassuring smile. "*Courage, mon ami*. This now rests in the King's good hands."

Hastening back to the Marais, Thierry felt as though something had exploded in his head. All the worries and fears he had been trying to suppress were like waters gushing from a broken dam. There was no containing them anymore. He realized that from the day he had witnessed the excavation of Montdidier's body to the dagger at his throat last evening, there had been a steady accumulation of evil. Now it was right in front of him: a tentacled, wispy presence that was alive—floating like mist, touching his face, his brain, threatening to engulf him.

DeNarsac's dreadful accusation of Macaire . . . was he correct? Surely not; not teasing, handsome, brave Macaire—Montdidier's cousin, their friend. Yet why would DeNarsac say such things? It was unlike him to pass judgment. Did he have reason to turn against Macaire? Envy of his new position? Jealousy? Thierry caught his breath. Lady Isabelle . . .

He knew DeNarsac loved her. Macaire certainly loved her. Denouncing Macaire would get rid of a rival. But DeNarsac was decent and kind—and yet . . . he was always so circumspect. Perhaps there was another side to him that Thierry had never seen. Was he hiding something? Was he scheming, manipulating, as others suggested? Did Thierry really know the man? He felt guilty conjuring such thoughts.

How would Isabelle take this latest news? She would be devastated, worried. What would the King decide about Dragon? Oh, gentle Dragon. The attempt to poison him had failed, but would someone try again? *Why* did Dragon attack Macaire? He remembered asking DeNarsac that very question last night. *Surely* not Macaire . . .

Thierry wondered if he would ever learn the truth

about anything. Would His Majesty know what to do? Even a King was only human. Could *anyone* sort out the confusion that was all around them? Adults had so many secrets.

He raced up the stairs of the townhouse to the private living quarters. The Count was sitting with Isabelle in his study, and they rose, concerned, as Thierry burst into the room.

"What is it, my dear?" Isabelle came to his side.

"What happened with His Majesty?" the Count asked quickly.

Thierry tried to speak coherently, but the words tumbling out of his mouth seemed a stream of nonsense. He couldn't decide what to reveal first: last night's episode, DeNarsac's horrifying accusation, or the King's request to see Dragon. Somehow the Count and Isabelle grasped what he was trying to say, and, though Isabelle looked shocked, they instantly took charge.

"It's all right, Thierry. I will accompany you and Dragon back to the Louvre," the Count said, and calling for Gilbert, he commanded him to ready the horses.

"I will come, too," said Isabelle. "Dear Thierry, this has been a dreadful ordeal—but we will be with you now."

The horses were brought around to the courtyard. Gilbert had saddled his own mount and leashed Dragon. The party of four, with the dog at Thierry's side, hastily departed, and within the hour they were entering the royal residence.

It was evident they were expected. Sentries waved them through, and doors opened for them as they approached. Two equerries escorted them through the palatial fortress, up the huge staircase, on toward the grand ballroom where the marvelous Feast of Saint Martin had been held. Thierry thought how different the world had been a mere three days ago.

Guards stood outside the towering portals, and as they were pulled wide, the small party drew back in astonishment. Every knight in the Court was assembled in the gilded hall, and all the lords, ladies, and attendants. At the far end, His Majesty King Charles V sat on his golden throne under the canopy. The Royal Astrologer, Thomas de Pizan, was on one side of him and Bureau de la Rivière on the other. Lady Béatrice was seated next to the Royal Chamberlain. DeNarsac stood nearby, looking miserable.

All eyes turned toward Thierry and Dragon, and there was complete silence. Surprised and dismayed, Thierry hesitated. The King raised his arm and beckoned him into the room.

Chapter Ten

THE TRIAL

 NTREZ! ENTREZ!" THE MONARCH called.

Thierry turned to the Count and Isabelle, uncertain.

The Count nodded reassuringly. "Do as he asks. We are with you."

"My dear Count, Isabelle. Pray take a seat. Thierry, bring the dog to me," His Majesty commanded.

Thierry walked with Dragon down the long corridor of people.

The King leaned forward and, with a gesture, indicated that Thierry should parade the dog in front of him. Dragon, alert and curious, pricked his ears. He behaved impeccably, pausing only to wag his tail enthusiastically when he saw DeNarsac. A ripple of charmed amusement came from the ladies present.

The King remarked, "He is indeed a splendid-looking animal. Now, Thierry, walk him along the line of knights assembled over there. Gentlemen!" he called to them. "Reach out to the dog as he passes. Extend a hand. Caress him."

The knights shifted nervously as Dragon approached, but they did as instructed. The dog responded to each man's overture with dignity, even delight. Clearly, he enjoyed the attention—the stroking, the scratching of his ears and chin. He occasionally glanced at Thierry for direction, but upon receiving the boy's encouraging nod, he moved on and was respectful and affectionate to everyone.

Thierry was so filled with pride, he thought his heart might burst. The King was nodding his approval. Almost imperceptibly, the monarch glanced toward Bureau de la Rivière—and the Chamberlain quietly signaled that two doors on the other side of the hall should be opened. Macaire was revealed standing behind them, talking with a young man of the Court. Seeing the large assembly in the ballroom, he hesitated, the smallest hint of bewilderment in his eyes. Then he smiled and entered, adopting his usual impudent swagger.

Dragon stiffened, and Thierry swiftly wound the leash around his hand—but still the dog pulled him almost the width of the vast room. Emitting the same harsh strangled sound as when he had last seen Macaire, Dragon scrambled toward the knight in a frenzy of rage. The immediate crowd pulled back in alarm. Béatrice screamed, and Isabelle rose to her feet, concerned. Two guards rushed to contain the dog and to block his access to Macaire.

"NO, Dragon! Cease now!" Thierry called firmly, and led the protesting animal to the other side of the room. The Court was alive with chatter, everyone amazed at the spectacle they had just witnessed. Glancing toward DeNarsac, Thierry saw that he was looking pained and anxious.

The King raised a hand for silence and called to Macaire.

"Apologies, dear Captain, for discomfiting you in this manner. It seemed the only way to confirm your allegations about the dog."

Macaire was red-faced and humiliated.

Béatrice stood up. "Now do you see what my son has

had to endure?" she cried. "I insist this vicious beast be dealt with at once!"

The King said crisply, "Madame, that is what we are *attempting* to do. If you will but seat yourself . . ." The monarch turned back to Macaire. "Indulge me just a moment more. Take this platter of meat and offer it to the dog."

A young page stepped forward holding a tray prepared with morsels of beef and venison.

Macaire's face registered disbelief.

"With respect, Your Majesty, is this necessary? Your brilliant strategy has allowed everyone to see the dog's animosity. Let us now spare the ladies present any further distress."

"More distressing would be to pronounce a royal edict too hastily. Pray proceed," the King commanded.

Angrily, Macaire took the platter and crossed the ballroom toward Dragon. The dog crouched, fangs bared. As Macaire placed the food a few feet from him, the dog lunged once more. Macaire retreated, and Thierry and the guards again restrained the animal. With a whine of frustration and anguish, Dragon settled on the floor. Head on his paws, eyes never wavering from Macaire, he completely ignored the repast before him.

His Majesty called, "Enough! Guards, you may remove the dog. Be sure that he comes to no harm. Thierry, remain with us a moment." Thierry moved to sit with Isabelle and the Count, while the King conferred quietly with Thomas de Pizan and Bureau de la Rivière. After a moment, he summoned Macaire and DeNarsac to come before him.

"Before I make judgment, the Court should hear your thoughts on this matter. These are unusual circumstances. Chevalier, do you have anything to say?"

Macaire said, "Your Majesty, I am sure there is a logical explanation. I have known the dog since he was a pup. I am a blood relative of his deceased master. We grew up together and were in each other's company more times than I can count. The dog never once behaved this way when Montdidier was alive. Two attacks on me—three, including today." He glanced at DeNarsac. "We can only wonder who or what has influenced the dog recently, and whom he will attack next."

The King turned expectantly toward DeNarsac. Watching the knight, Thierry sensed his turmoil. Would he reiterate in front of the entire Court the words he had spoken earlier to His Majesty? DeNarsac glanced at Isabelle. She was sitting erect, looking pale and worried, her restless hands betraying the anxiety she was feeling.

The knight's face was etched with sorrow as he turned to Macaire.

"I know that my words will cause irreparable damage between us, and may even promote consequences beyond that. But someone has to consider the rights of our friend, the late Aubrey de Montdidier. I, too, grew up with him, and never was there a more virtuous knight. Since his demise, I have come to equally appreciate and trust the honor and integrity of his noble hound." DeNarsac paused and took a deep breath. "What has happened here today, in addition to the two previous attacks upon you, has fueled my conviction that Dragon holds the memory of something deeply disturbing to him . . . something in which you played a part. I reluctantly conclude that you were involved in the assassination of your cousin."

A hissing intake of breath rippled through the Court. Macaire looked stunned.

DeNarsac continued.

"This magnificent dog, Montdidier's loyal companion, has spoken three times in the only way he can." Turning to the King, DeNarsac said, "Your Majesty, on behalf of Aubrey de Montdidier and this noble hound, I respectfully request that justice prevail."

Isabelle's hands fluttered to her face. Lady Béatrice swayed and leaned against Bureau de la Rivière for support.

Macaire gasped. "Shall a soldier of the King be accused by a mere beast?" Appalled, he distanced himself from DeNarsac. "I cannot believe that you would slander me thus—a man whom I have called friend, whom I have known all my life, whom I have loved dearly. *Nom de Dieu*, Guy—tell me you are not in your right mind and I will try to understand and forgive this madness."

DeNarsac remained silent.

Contemptuously, Macaire said, "So be it! It is not in *my* nature to discredit any man, but since you have opened this pit of worms, I confess—with shame, I might add—that I have harbored suspicions about *you*; that it is *your* savagery that has influenced Dragon. I think *you* perpetrated the dreadful deed upon my beloved cousin! We have only your word, and that of your young squire, that the dog led you to his grave. I have been wickedly

maligned and mistreated today. I, too, demand justice."
Macaire gave a bitter laugh. "But since you have poisoned
the minds of all here, can there be anyone left to give fair
judgment?"

There was no sound in the great hall—not a single
movement among the hushed assembly.

The King said firmly, "Indeed there is someone." He
rose to his feet. "There is the judgment of God. He will
aid the cause of the innocent and bring down the guilty.
I propose a duel between accuser and accused."

"*Vous avez bien dit*, Your Majesty," Macaire proclaimed. "It is the only honorable solution and I welcome
it." He faced DeNarsac, his eyes blazing, his face flushed.
"I will meet you anywhere, any time. The sooner the
better."

"As you wish," DeNarsac replied evenly. "You have
only to name the form of combat."

"The form of combat has been decided," the King
stated irritably, "if you will *allow* me to finish. . . . The day
after tomorrow, on the Île Nôtre Dame, at the Campus
Rosaeus beside the Cathedral, Richard Macaire,
Chevalier and Captain of the Royal Guard, will take arms
against the defender of Aubrey de Montdidier—the

wolfhound Dragon."

The Court erupted in astonishment. Isabelle cried out. Béatrice swooned.

The King raised his voice above the din.

"The accused, Richard Macaire, and his accuser, the dog Dragon, will be placed under separate guard until noon on Wednesday. Sieur DeNarsac will also remain in our custody. That is all." He stepped down from the dais and made for the doors, his attendants scrambling to go before him to ensure his smooth passage out of the hall.

Thierry ran to DeNarsac as guards prepared to escort him and Macaire to their chambers of detention.

"Oh, Guy! This is terrible! Is there anything I can do?"

"Stay close to Gilbert. Do not be alone. Look after Lady Isabelle."

"Will Dragon be all right, do you suppose? Will you?"

"I think he will be safe. I shall be fine."

Isabelle caught his arm as he passed.

"What have you done?" she cried. "What good can come of this? It will not bring Aubrey back . . ."

Aching with sorrow, DeNarsac replied, "Madame,

you know Dragon as well as I. And you know me. Why would either of us risk breaking so many hearts? I, too, stand to lose everything I hold dear. But Montdidier was unjustly slain, and for his sake I am driven to speak the truth."

DeNarsac was led from the hall. Isabelle brushed away the sudden rush of tears, and Thierry placed his hand in hers. Béatrice was sobbing, and they moved to console her.

"Aunt, come home now. We will take comfort from each other," Isabelle said gently.

"There is no comfort," Béatrice moaned. "Except in vindication. But what can a woman do? One cannot alter the ways of men or God."

The family returned to the Marais house, the Count leading the way, a lone figure lost in thought. He wondered at the curse that had befallen his family: the deaths of his beloved wife and Thierry's parents, then his nephew, and now the attempted assassination of DeNarsac and Dragon. Life seemed merely a battle for survival, and he felt old and helpless.

Béatrice and Isabelle were silent, but Thierry and Gilbert spoke quietly and urgently to each other. Would Dragon be safe? How could a dog fight a duel? What form would the combat take on Wednesday? What were DeNarsac and Macaire thinking as they waited, confined in their quarters?

"How do you suppose the King arrived at this solution?" Thierry asked.

"It must have been Thomas de Pizan's idea," Gilbert replied. "It is his style . . . and the King has such faith in his guidance."

"I wonder if he can foretell whom the stars will favor," Thierry mused. "It is certainly an unusual edict."

"And yet it is just, for Dragon made the first accusation," Gilbert countered, then asked breathlessly, "Thierry, do you believe that Macaire slew Montdidier?"

"I do not wish to believe it. But if he did not, then Dragon is reckless and DeNarsac ruthless and dishonest. . . ."

They were silent a moment. Thierry suddenly said, "Did you notice Lieutenant Landry was not in the hall?"

"Yes. I inquired about him," Gilbert replied. "I was

told he is in the infirmary. I know not why."

They rode on, each preoccupied, aware that questions only led to further questions.

That evening, Lady Béatrice confronted the Count.

"Gilles, you must intercede with His Majesty on Richard's behalf. He will listen to you, I am sure. This travesty demeans us all, and is utterly *bizarre*."

The Count frowned and rubbed a hand against his temple.

"Madame, I think it unwise to challenge the authority of the King."

"But it is your responsibility. DeNarsac is in your service and you are accountable for his actions. Would you place loyalty to him before your own flesh and blood? Richard is not only my son, but *your* nephew."

"What of Montdidier?" the Count replied sadly. "He was my nephew also, and was to be my son-in-law."

"The devil take you, sir!" Béatrice turned away in disgust. "I am surrounded by spineless men."

Isabelle and Thierry had been listening to the exchange, and she rose to Béatrice's defense.

"Father, I must agree with Aunt. *Something* has to be

done to halt this madness. I have buried one love as a result of violence. Must we now endure more? The prospect of this fight is unbearable. Surely there can be a peaceful solution? And what of Dragon? Should he even survive on Wednesday, it can only breed more viciousness in him. Then there is DeNarsac. His life will also be in question if he is proved wrong."

The Count sighed wearily. "I will do what I can."

The following morning, Thierry asked if he might accompany the Count and Gilbert to the Palace.

"While you seek audience with His Majesty, I may be permitted to see Dragon," he reasoned. "He must surely be wondering why we have abandoned him, and I want to be sure he is safe."

The Count was preoccupied and nodded his assent.

Dragon was ecstatic when he saw Thierry. As the boy enfolded him, the dog licked his face, snuffling and whimpering with delight. He pranced about and ran expectantly to the door of the cell that imprisoned him.

"Alas, Dragon, I am not here to release you." Thierry felt a catch in his throat. "But I can stay with you awhile and we will see each other tomorrow." He lovingly patted his friend and caressed his rough fur. Dragon pressed against him, and each took comfort and strength from the other.

Gilbert had been attending the Count upstairs, but now he appeared and joined Thierry in Dragon's cell.

"My master has received permission to speak with His Majesty. He requests that we return to him within the half hour." He stroked Dragon gently. "How sad this all is. I wish there were something we could do."

Thierry said thoughtfully, "There is perhaps *one* thing. Come with me."

They took their leave of the dog. Thierry explained to the guards, "He is a splendid fellow and not vicious at all. Please be gentle with him."

"Where are we going?" Gilbert inquired as soon as they were out of earshot.

"To the infirmary," Thierry replied. "Since Landry is there, he may not be aware of what transpired yesterday. He might provide some morsel of information that will be useful to us."

"For example?"

"I'm not sure. . . . Perhaps he can tell us more about

Macaire on the morning of Montdidier's disappearance. He may confirm some rift between them, which would suggest a motive. . . ."

"It's unlikely he'll even see us," Gilbert countered.

"It's worth a try."

Thierry stopped to look around. "But how to find the infirmary?"

"Oh, that is the easy part. Watch this." Gilbert approached a sentry. "Sirrah, we have a message from the Count of Montargis for a friend in the sick bay. The Count awaits his reply. Kindly point us in the right direction."

Within minutes, they were standing before a formidable-looking nun in charge of the infirmary ward. Gilbert's tone was respectful and courteous.

"Good morning, Sister. We have a message for Lieutenant Landry from his Captain, the Chevalier Macaire. We would like a moment with him, if possible?"

"Why, yes, he is in the other room." She pointed.

"God bless you, good lady." Gilbert grinned at Thierry as they moved away. "Now, lad, the rest is up to you."

Landry was lying on a cot, looking flushed and feverish. He was shivering beneath a crude blanket.

"Do you suppose it is safe to approach him?" Thierry asked, alarmed.

"Of course, else we would never have been allowed to see him," Gilbert said reassuringly.

"Lieutenant, it is Thierry and Gilbert. We are here on behalf of the Count, who wishes to know how you fare."

Landry started at sight of them. He seemed unsure who his visitors were.

"Uh—*bien. Très bien.* I shall be on my feet shortly," he mumbled, his voice slurred. Thierry realized that the young man had been sedated, and he felt disappointment. There was no sense questioning him in his present condition.

Gilbert was saying, ". . . an unpleasant situation for you, sir."

Landry closed his eyes briefly, then opened them and tried to focus on his guests. "It is merely an ague, a sudden attack. One moment I was healthy, the next . . ."

Thierry said, "Do you have need of anything? The Count wishes you to be as comfortable as possible."

"*Non, non,* I will be good as new—perhaps on the morrow." He closed his eyes again.

Thierry glanced at Gilbert and shrugged his shoulders. As they walked away, the kindly nun bustled toward them.

"Au revoir, et merci!" Gilbert bowed.

"Que Dieu vous accompagne," she said, smiling.

"Lieutenant Landry seems very ill," Thierry commented to her.

She nodded. "It will take a long time to heal. The bite has festered and there is serious infection."

Thierry felt as though someone had hit him in the stomach. He was suddenly weak, and nausea washed over him. He leaned against the stone wall for support.

"What is the matter?" Gilbert asked, concerned.

"I need but a moment." Thierry waited for the bile to subside, then said, "Gilbert, I beg a favor. Do not question me now, but return to Landry and simply inform him that you have retrieved his *sword*. If he asks how, say only that it fell into your hands. Please do this for me. It is of great importance that I know his answer. I will wait outside."

Gilbert looked at him, puzzled. Then he turned on his heel and went back into the ward.

Thierry drew in deep breaths of fresh air. It must have been Landry who attacked DeNarsac two nights ago. . . . Hadn't DeNarsac said he almost recognized the voice? But was Landry acting on Macaire's behalf? And had he tried to poison Dragon? Thierry wiped his damp forehead. The questions were relentless.

Within moments, Gilbert returned.

"What did he say?" Thierry demanded.

"I don't know what you expected, but he seemed— unsure, somehow, surprised. He did ask how I obtained the sword. When I said what you told me to say, he replied that it had been stolen from him. He mentioned being in a tavern when it was taken and added that was probably where he had contracted his illness."

"Thank you, Gilbert."

"Is it what you needed to know?" the squire asked.

"Yes, it helps a great deal. I will tell you everything, I promise, but let us now return for the Count, before he becomes worried about us."

The Count was sitting outside the royal apartments, elbows on his knees, his head in his hands. One look at his dejected manner, and Thierry and Gilbert knew that he had been unsuccessful in his attempt to sway the King.

Chapter Eleven

THE COMBAT

HROUGHOUT THE NIGHT, THIERRY was rest-less. Sleep had eluded him of late, and once again it was denied him.

He wished he knew the wisest thing to do. If he told the Count, or even the King, they would need to speak to Landry—but Landry would assuredly deny every-thing. Macaire would deny any knowledge of Landry's involvement. Landry claimed his sword had been stolen . . . and what if that were true? Could the bite he had sustained be a mere coincidence? Certainly he would claim it was. It was all so complicated!

Then suddenly it came to him with simplicity and clarity: The answer lay with Dragon. He had assaulted Macaire three times, and he would not have done so without good reason. The dog knew the truth, and he had indicted Macaire. Landry's involvement was a secondary issue. True, the sword was his . . . but the only unanswered questions were: had he used it the night of the attempted assassination, or had it been stolen from him and used by someone else—and was he in league with Macaire? Perhaps *both* men had been involved in the murder of Montdidier, and all the subsequent acts that had followed. But *why*?

He shivered. As dawn began to appear at his window, he went to a bowl and dashed his face with water. He wished he could speak with DeNarsac. He wondered what he was doing this very moment. And Macaire? And Dragon? Thierry sank to his knees and whispered a prayer.

Paris was shrouded with fog that morning, and the city appeared mysterious and forbidding.

The Count and his party departed early for the Campus Rosaeus. Béatrice was fraught with worry and desperate to see her son. Isabelle would have preferred to stay home but realized that her family needed her. She looked drawn and anxious, her cloak pulled close about her.

Gilbert spurred his horse to catch up with Thierry

and, with a jerk of his head, indicated he wished to speak with him privately.

As they moved away from the group, the squire said urgently, "Thierry, I have news. Something you said yesterday remained with me. Before saddling the horses this morning, I spoke with Jacques, the head groom. After Montdidier's disappearance, our inquiries concerned only *him*. It never occurred to us to ask who *else* had been out that fateful morning of the joust. . . ."

Thierry held his breath.

Gilbert continued. "Jacques remembered that when he came down to the stables that day, several other horses were missing from their stalls. Among them were those belonging to Macaire and Landry."

Thierry closed his eyes. Memories of last June were as clear as if they had occurred yesterday. . . . Macaire saying, "Marry, but I'm travel sore! I had a fitful night and I could not wake this morning. . . ."

The boy felt sick at heart as he contemplated the deception and lies that had led to this moment.

As they crossed the bridge to the Ile Nôtre Dame, many people were moving in the same direction. Their numbers swelled as they neared the Campus Rosaeus.

How had word of the duel spread so quickly? Thierry sensed that people were excited and in a festive mood, anticipating a day that would probably be one of the most unusual they would ever witness. What would the outcome be? Would Macaire prevail? Would Dragon survive? If Dragon were vanquished, what would happen to DeNarsac?

They approached the field, and Thierry saw that it had been ringed with posts like a huge stockade. A tide of humanity poured in through the gates: knights, lords, ladies, the clergy, and especially the lower classes. Pickpockets were going about their seamy business, wagers were being taken. There were children, scruffy urchins, beggars.

Still the fog hung low, and with it an odd, unseasonable heat—damp, and pressing close. It was difficult to breathe. They left the horses with a groom outside the arena and pushed through the jostling throng to a section that had been roped off for the elite of the Court. Thierry put his arm protectively about Isabelle, and she clung to him fiercely.

Trumpeters and heralds appeared. There was a stir among the crowd as DeNarsac and Macaire were brought out, each escorted by members of the King's Guard. They were Macaire's own men, and they could not look at him.

Thierry tried to read DeNarsac's expression but could not. Turning to Isabelle, he said, "Forgive me . . . I must go to him." He elbowed through the crush of people, twisting, dodging, pushing, until he reached the barrier that prevented public entry onto the field.

"Guy! Guy! Over here!" he yelled, waving furiously. The knight did not hear him, and Thierry cupped his hands and called again as loudly as he could. "DeNarsac! Over *here*!"

The knight glanced around, and their eyes met. DeNarsac frowned, then smiled and raised a hand. It was a sad gesture somehow, and Thierry felt tears coursing down his cheeks. He realized it would be impossible to impart his news of Landry and Macaire. In any case, nothing could be done about it now.

He tried to smile bravely and held up his thumbs as if to ask if DeNarsac was all right. The knight responded, nodding, and Thierry made a little gesture of prayer.

Trumpets rang out—a hollow sound in the dense mist. His Majesty swept onto the field with a large party of guests, their colorful attire sparkling like jewels in the drab gray of the morning. The King acknowledged the applause from the crowd, and climbed the stairs to the royal enclosure.

Thierry saw Macaire bow his head to Isabelle, his hand against his heart as if trying to rise above the indignity of this day. It was the same gesture he had made five months ago at the tournament, before the world had changed so tragically. Isabelle looked anguished, and as Thierry fought his way back to her, he tried to push down the fear and dread that were rising in his heart. If only it would all go away, if only he could wake up and find himself in Montargis once more with Isabelle, Montdidier, Dragon, Macaire, DeNarsac, friends as before . . . then this would simply be another of his terrible nightmares.

A Marshal and eight soldiers of the King's Guard walked onto the field, the latter placing themselves at various points around the circle of combat. A stout wooden barrel, open at either end, was carried out and placed on the muddied grass. Macaire was escorted to the Marshal's side. A shield was looped over the knight's left arm, and a mace—a mean-looking weapon with an ovate, spiked head—was placed in his right hand.

The trumpets sounded once more and Dragon was brought out. A heavy circlet was around his neck and he was leashed with chains. The onlookers roared at the sight of him. Dragon seemed bewildered, but when he spied Macaire, his fur bristled and he crouched, straining to be free of the guards who held him.

The Marshal called for order, his voice resonating around the arena.

"*Citoyens de Paris!* We are gathered to witness the trial by combat between the accuser, the hound Dragon, and the accused, the Chevalier Macaire. Weapons allowed this day shall be the mace provided for Macaire versus the natural defenses of the beast. Protection shall be the shield for the knight, and the barrel for the dog, into which he may withdraw. Let all present see that no injustice is done!"

The Marshal bowed to the King. The monarch raised his hand, and as he brought it down, Dragon was released. Immediately, he launched himself at Macaire. The knight swung at him viciously, and the mace connected with Dragon's shoulder, bowling him over and over in the grass like a deer that had been felled. Thierry gasped, and Isabelle turned away, unable to watch.

Scrambling unsteadily to his feet and shaking his head, Dragon retreated to size up his opponent. Skirting him, ducking out of the way of the swinging club, the dog looked for his best opportunity, darting left and right, forward and back. With awe, Thierry realized that Dragon was using the fencing skills he had learned as a pup when playfully sparring with Montdidier. Fangs bared, lips curled, Dragon baited his adversary, daring him to come at him.

Macaire renewed his attack. Lunging forward, he suddenly missed his footing, falling to one knee. Seizing the moment, Dragon rushed in, only to twist away, howling in pain. A red stain appeared on his white fur, and a roar erupted from the populace as they realized first blood had been drawn.

Glancing toward DeNarsac, Thierry saw a look of consternation on his face. The dog had sustained a large cut on his shoulder.

Trying to rid himself of the pain, Dragon licked his wound. Macaire took the advantage to swing at him once more, connecting with another powerful hit. The dog's legs buckled, and Thierry buried his face in Isabelle's cloak, choking with sobs.

Dragon lurched toward the barrel, crawling inside it to avoid the punishing blows. Macaire placed his foot upon the timbers and with a strong thrust set the barrel in motion, rolling it over and over. Unable to gain purchase, the dog was tumbled about. The knight continued his assault, pushing and kicking mercilessly, swinging the mace against the open end of the barrel, forcing the confused Dragon to exit the other side and come onto the field once more.

Legs trembling, eyes bloodshot, the dog stumbled around the knight, appearing to take refuge behind him. As Macaire spun, so Dragon again ran behind, repeating the maneuver until the knight became disoriented and could do nothing but continually glance over his shoulder.

Attempting to swing the mace in a backward arc, he left his shield arm vulnerable. Darting forward, Dragon sank his teeth into the fleshy muscle just above Macaire's elbow. The knight's head snapped back in pain, and he doubled forward, then back again, trying to rid himself of the animal's agonizing grip. The crowd was cheering, hats were being thrown, fists were pumping the air.

Dragon refused to let go. His wound gushing, his hind legs struggling for traction, he was dragged this way and that, oblivious to the club that continued to swing with horrifying force against him.

Man and dog were at an impasse—frozen in equal strength. But ultimately the pain became too much for Macaire. He dropped the shield—and with it something that glinted on the earth before being kicked away in the scuffle.

Thierry gasped, as did the crowd, and now their blood lust turned to fury as they realized that the knight had been concealing a dagger, and that he had used it to generate the wound on Dragon's shoulder.

The dog released his grip and came around to face Macaire once again. The knight's left arm hung limply at his side, but the mace was still in his right hand. With almost superhuman strength, he lashed out, swinging left and right, forcing Dragon to retreat into the barrel once more. This time there was no escape, for it had rolled against the side of the arena and was firmly pinned there.

With the crowd screaming, Macaire accelerated his attack, pounding at the wood, splintering the timbers with each blow.

Thierry could bear it no longer.

"*Nom de Dieu!*" he sobbed, his fists against his face.

"*Arrêtez!* Stop! Stop!" He glanced in anguish at the Count. "Tell His Majesty he *has* to intercede!" he implored.

The Count gently placed an arm around the boy's shoulder.

"Thierry, the outcome decides the innocence or guilt," he said somberly.

Thierry looked toward DeNarsac and saw him struggling with his guards in an attempt to free himself and get to Dragon. The boy tore from the Count's embrace and thrust into the crowd once again, pushing toward the barrier. He glimpsed Macaire's face, maniacal with intent, and saw him strike the barrel so hard that it would need only one more hit for the frame to shatter completely and for Dragon's life to be ended.

Macaire raised his arm for the final blow, hefting it a fraction higher for greatest impact. In that moment, Dragon flew from the battered enclosure with the last strength he could muster and connected with the body of his adversary. Macaire tumbled backward and hit the earth with such force that the wind was knocked out of him. Gasping, trying desperately to suck air into his lungs, the knight could only claw ineffectually at the dog. Dragon straddled him, pinning him to the ground. A collective intake of breath rose from the crowded arena; then, suddenly, all was silent and still.

His senses reeling, Macaire saw the dog's fangs, dripping with blood, just inches from his face and felt Dragon's hot breath upon his throat. It seemed that the animal's head metamorphosed in the fog, undulating, receding, then reappearing as a new and more terrifying apparition. With a rasping intake of breath, Macaire's voice was shrill as he screamed:

"Montdidier! Forgive me! I have sinned against you!"

Dragon's teeth closed about Macaire's jugular, almost but not quite piercing the skin. As a great sigh went up from the populace, another voice rang out clearly.

"NO, DRAGON! HOLD! NO MORE NOW! CEASE!"

Thierry was hardly aware that he had shouted the words, but Dragon heard him and looked up, trying to place the boy's whereabouts.

The King signaled swiftly. The guards closed in to enchain the dog once more and to pull him off Macaire. The knight rolled onto his side, his knees drawn up to his chest.

DeNarsac broke from the men restraining him and ran across the field. Thierry scrambled over the railings and dropped onto the ground below. Both reached Dragon at the same moment and enfolded him, caressing him, soothing him, patting him, stanching his wounds with gentle hands.

DeNarsac released the bindings from the dog's neck and indicated that the guards should turn their attention to Macaire. The King beckoned, and the fallen knight was brought before him and thrust to his knees.

Béatrice was wailing in grief and horror. "Your Majesty, be merciful, I beg you!"

Raising a hand for silence, King Charles V announced solemnly, "It is the judgment of God. The royal edict will be posted at dawn tomorrow. Take the offender away."

As the guards escorted the beaten Macaire off the field, they passed DeNarsac and Thierry. Lifting his head, DeNarsac met Macaire's eyes and their gaze held.

"Why?" he asked quietly.

Hesitating a mere fraction of a second, Macaire shrugged and, with a catch in his voice, replied simply and chillingly, "He owned the world."

Isabelle and Gilbert came running across the field with dressings and water for Dragon. The hound lay on his side, too exhausted to move. As they tended his wounds, Isabelle glanced at DeNarsac, her face flushed. Then she turned to Thierry and patted his hand lovingly.

"You did well," she said quietly.

DeNarsac smiled at him. "Indeed you did, Thierry. Today you spoke with Montdidier's voice, and surely he watched over Dragon. He was with us all."

Chapter 12

THE CONCLUSION

HARLES V KEPT HIS word, and in May he came to Montargis for a royal visit.

Thierry accompanied the King, the Count, and DeNarsac on a morning ride through the spring countryside and thought that it had never seemed more green, more beautiful. Pink and white blossoms drifted from the trees like snow, and lilies of the valley and bluebells bloomed beneath the woodland canopy.

Dragon, his health now fully restored, loped contentedly beside the riders. The royal retinue followed several paces behind, armor glinting, banners waving in the sun.

"I am so very pleased to make this visit, Gilles." The King stretched in his saddle. "The country air is always so beneficial, not only for *la goutte* but also for the spirit."

"The pleasure is ours, Sire," the Count replied. "May

I extend my gratitude once again for your proposed improvements to the château."

"We will begin as soon as possible." The King nodded. "I may also install a clock in the tower. It will chime every quarter hour—it brings marvelous order to daily living." He called over his shoulder. "Thierry!" The boy spurred his mount to ride beside him. "How fortunate that we are here for your birthday, my young friend! Tonight our celebrations will join with yours."

"Your Majesty," Thierry replied breathlessly, "it is a birthday I will never forget. The illuminated book you so kindly gave me will be cherished always."

"Good, good." The King turned to the Count. "This is a brave young man, Gilles. He will make an excellent knight. But see that he attends the university as well. A fine mind should not be wasted."

"Of course, Sire."

The King turned to DeNarsac.

"*Alors, Monsieur le Capitaine.* I have been thinking a great deal about you since last we met in Paris. At the suggestion of the Count, it delights me to recognize your courage and integrity by conferring upon you the title of Viscount de Montargis, second only to your master and to his estates. We will make it official on the morrow."

DeNarsac looked startled, then bowed his head.

"Your Majesty, I am deeply honored." He turned to the Count. "My lord, I am grateful. But you had no need . . ."

"But I, too, am grateful. Without you and Thierry, the mystery of Montdidier's death might never have been solved, and I shudder to think of the consequences that could have followed."

"Don't forget Dragon," Thierry added quietly. "Without him, we would never have known where to begin."

The King nodded. "We shall never forget Dragon. Forevermore, people will be telling his story . . . and it will become legend."

The Forest of Bondy loomed before them, and the men fell silent for a while, each lost in contemplation of the brutal murder that had taken place there so many months ago.

Then the King spoke again. "In his confession, the Chevalier Macaire revealed that he was able to entice Dragon into the forest by slaying a deer and leaving a bloodied trail that the dog could not resist. When Dragon didn't return, Montdidier went in to find him—enabling

Macaire and Landry to carry out the dreadful deed."

De Narsac said thoughtfully, "Even with such temptation, Your Majesty, I feel certain that Dragon would have heeded Montdidier's call, as he always did . . . but for the fact that he sensed Macaire was there."

"I would imagine so," the monarch concurred. "We learned that Macaire used the very dagger he brought forth so illegally at the Campus Rosaeus. Dragon tried to come to Montdidier's aid, but when they attempted to kill him as well, the brave fellow escaped. He presumably observed the burial from a hidden vantage point, and kept vigil there until he felt it was safe to come to you."

"It is still difficult to believe," the Count remarked bitterly. "My own nephew, my sister's son . . . how could he have carried such venom, such ambition and envy for so many years, without any of us realizing it?"

"Very little surprises me anymore," the monarch replied soberly. "So often within a family, we see only what we wish to see, *n'est-ce pas?*"

"I doubt I will ever understand it," the Count said. "But your sentence was merciful, Sire."

"Truth be told, our motive was twofold," the King acknowledged wryly. "Stripping the man of his title and banishing him to Rhodes was hardly punishment enough for such a heinous crime. But he will be an asset to the *Hospitaliers*. And upholding poverty, chastity, and obedience may well be the harshest sentence of all."

"Your Majesty, if I might ask a question?" Thierry spoke.

"Mais oui."

"Was Lieutenant Landry ever found?"

The King shook his head.

"Ah, non. He escaped from the infirmary the day of the duel. Your visit surely caused him great anxiety. Of course, he was fevered and had infection. He may well be deceased by now. . . ."

Thierry gazed heavenward, wondering if Landry was alive and, if so, where he might have gone. A hawk was circling above him in the azure expanse, seeking its prey. The bird's head was clearly defined, and the soft, feathered tips of its vast wingspan rippled in the air currents upon which it soared.

Later in the day, Isabelle asked DeNarsac and Thierry to walk with her and Dragon by the river.

"Guy . . ." Isabelle said haltingly. "I have apologized

for my demeanor toward you in Paris, but it haunts me still. I would never knowingly cause anyone pain, let alone a man as decent as you."

DeNarsac reached above him and casually plucked a sprig from a cherry tree laden with blossom. Thierry sensed the knight's awkwardness as he searched for appropriate words. The boy wondered if he should retreat and allow the conversation to unfold privately—but DeNarsac replied simply, "I understand. I always have." He handed Isabelle the cluster of flowers.

"You are very generous," she replied. "How appalling it is that one man's evil act could taint so many hearts. He implied many dreadful things. I did not know whom or what to believe."

The truth of her words surprised Thierry. He realized that even he, for a time, had doubted DeNarsac's integrity . . . in spite of all he had witnessed, all he had shared with the man. It seemed impossible now.

"I have wondered these past months when it was that Macaire made the terrible decision to—to take my beloved's life." Isabelle gently touched the blossom in her hands.

The knight replied thoughtfully, "I suspect, my Lady, it was after he received news of your betrothal. We know he was ambitious. He must have felt that Montdidier had everything that he, Macaire, desired to obtain—property, position, and ultimately the woman he loved. One can only guess at the effort it took to maintain a demeanor that charmed us all."

Isabelle looked away, her eyes glistening.

"It may seem strange, but I am grateful that the King spared Macaire's life. I could not bear one more senseless death in the family." She brushed a hand across her eyes. "Did His Majesty say how long he would be visiting with us?"

"Two more days at least," DeNarsac replied. "He is looking forward to tonight's feast in his honor, and to celebrating Thierry's birthday. You seem to be his new favorite, lad—what a conceit you will have!"

"Not at all!" Isabelle hugged Thierry. "We cannot have too much to celebrate. Heaven knows it is time for some joy!"

"Guy," Thierry said shyly, "have you shared the news of your appointment?"

Isabelle stopped walking and turned to DeNarsac, her face suddenly grave.

"What news?"

"My Lady, this morning His Majesty conferred upon me the title of Viscount. I shall be assisting your father." Color flushed in the knight's cheeks.

"But this is wonderful!" Isabelle clapped her hands with delight. "For a moment I feared you had been transferred to Paris."

"Au contraire, Madame." DeNarsac smiled. "You will likely be thoroughly tired of me in a matter of weeks."

"I doubt that. It will be a great pleasure to work with you." Her eyes fixed on his a moment, and she added, "I have much need of your friendship."

The knight struggled to find the words that filled his heart.

"My Lady, the need is mutual. As long as I draw breath, I swear you will never be abandoned again."

Thierry suddenly felt that the world had shifted and that balance had finally been restored. He picked up a stick for Dragon and threw it as far as he could. It fell into the gently flowing river, and the magnificent hound raced after it and delightedly plunged in to retrieve it.

Bounding back, he shook himself, and sparkling drops of water flew in all directions, showering them all. They laughed, and he frolicked about, nudging them, brushing them gently, reveling in the affection of the three people he loved most . . . happy they were at his side.

FIN

THE LEGEND

To affirm the nobleness of hounds I shall tell
a tale of a hound, that of Aubrey de
Montdider, the which men may see painted
in the realm of France in many places.

That Aubrey was a knight of the King's house of
France, and upon a day he was riding past the
woods of Bondy, and led with him the said Dragon
that he had nourished up. A man that ran upon him

wood and slew him without warning. . . .

When the hound sought his master and found
him dead, and when he had been for three days
and might no longer bide for hunger, he returned
again to Court, and there he found his master's
friend

let him

The King of France, the which was wise and
perceiving, commanded that the hound and made

EDMUND DE LANGLEY
Duke of York, 1341–1402

FRENCH-ENGLISH GLOSSARY

à la mode—in fashion

alors—well now

arrêtez—stop

au contraire—on the contrary

au revoir—good-bye

bien sûr—of course

bonjour—hello

bon sang!—wow! (literally: "Good blood!")

brigand—thug, criminal

Capitaine—Captain

C'est vrai—It's true

chère/cher—dear

citoyens de Paris—citizens of Paris

Connétable—Constable

consommé—broth

coup—brilliant feat (literally: "cut")

Courage, mon ami—Courage, my friend

Dame—Lady

Dites-lui!—Tell him!

élégants—bluebloods, aristocrats

en route—on the way

Entrez!—Enter!

et—and

Fin—The End

fleur-de-lis—lily, the flower and symbol of France

la goutte—gout

Grace à Dieu—Thanks be to God

hélas—alas

Hospitaliers—A religious military service (formerly
        Knights of Malta) organized during the
        Middle Ages to care for the sick and needy

île—island

le Jacquerie—a 1358 peasant uprising against the
        nobility

Laissez aller!—Let them go!

madame—lady, my lady

mais—but

mêlée—brawl, battle, contest

merci—thank you

mesdames—ladies

mon ami—my friend

mon cher—my dear

mon Dieu—my God

Monsieur—Mister

N'est-ce pas?—Isn't that so?

nom de Dieu—in the name of God

nom d'un nom—in the name of God (variation) (literally: "name of a name")

non—no

oui—yes

par Dieu—by God

par le ciel—by Heaven

Que Dieu vous accompagne—May the lord be with you

Quel plaisir!—What a pleasure!

la rage—rabies

ravissante—ravishing

superbe—superb

Tiens, mon brave!—Stay, my brave one!

très bien—very well

Les Trois Rois—The Three Kings

Vous avez bien dit—Well said

vraiment—truly, really

GLOSSARY OF MEDIEVAL TERMS

ague—fever, chills

balsam—aromatic plant resin, oil, or fluid

Black Death—The Plague

burghers—inhabitants of a borough or town; middle-class citizens

cantle—the upward-curving rear part of a saddle

caparison—an ornamented covering or cloak for a horse

cassock—a long vestment or robe worn as an outer garment by clergymen

destrier—a war horse, charger

doublet—a man's close-fitting jacket or vest

ecclesiastics—members of the clergy or church

equerries—officers in personal service to a member of the royal family

ewer—a large water pitcher

falchion—a medieval sword with a short, broad, slightly curved blade

filial—of or due from a son or daughter

fistulous—of or like a fistula—an opening in the surface of the body created as a result of a wound, abscess, or the like; a surgically created passage made for drainage

frumenty—wheat pudding, boiled with milk, currants, raisins, and spices

garrison—a military post, a fortified place with troops

helm—helmet

hose—a tight-fitting men's outer garment covering hips, legs, and feet, and attaching to the doublet by cords or ribbons

humors—the four fluids formerly considered responsible for one's health and disposition: blood (buoyancy), phlegm (apathy), black bile (melancholy), and yellow bile (choler)

jennet—a lady's horse

jesses—straps fastened around a falcon's leg, with a ring at one end for attaching a leash

lance—a light spear; a long wooden shaft with a sharp metal spearhead

lists—a high fence of stakes enclosing the area for a tournament; any place of combat or contest

litter—a stretcher for carrying the sick or wounded

livery—uniform

lute—a stringed instrument related to the guitar, with a body shaped like half a pear and with six to thirteen strings

mail—flexible body armor made of small overlapping metal rings or loops of chain

midsummer—the summer solstice

page—a boy between the ages of seven and thirteen in training for knighthood, often in attendance upon ladies or persons of high rank

palfrey—a well-bred, easy-paced saddle horse

palisade—a fence of large, pointed stakes

pallet—a small bed or straw-filled sleeping pad, used directly on the floor

pantler—the staff member responsible for keeping the pantry stocked

reeds—rustic musical instruments made from hollow stems or stalks, played by blowing

retainers—attendants, servants, especially to someone of rank

rouncey—a strong but less well-bred horse for squires and retainers

scepter—a rod or staff, highly ornamented, held by a ruler on ceremonial occasions as a symbol of sovereignty

sentry—guard, watchman

solstice—the annual date when the sun reaches its maximum distance north or south of the celestial equator; summer solstice, June 21, marks the beginning of summer and the longest day (or period of sunlight) of the year, and is often celebrated with festivals, fairs, and harvest feasts. In Europe it is/was often referred to as "midsummer," as it is the middle of the growing season.

squire—a young man of high birth, fourteen or more years of age, attending or in apprenticeship to a knight

tallow—cattle or sheep fat used in making candles and soaps

tanner—a leather maker

taper—a candle; a long wick coated with wax and used for lighting other candles, lamps, etc.

tinderbox—a box for holding flammable material, flint, and steel for starting a fire

tippet—a long, hanging part of a hood, cape, or sleeve

trencher—a kind of plate made out of a slab of old brown bread, slightly hollowed in the middle, into which was put meat or other food; a board or platter on which to serve food

tunic—a padded robe or garment worn underneath armor to absorb blows

vespers—evening prayers

The authors extend heartfelt gratitude to the following people for their contribution to this book:

Nadia Margolis and Kelly DeVries, for their expertise and knowledge of the period and for their guidance, support, and fact checking

Francine Taylor, for her tireless research (for which we also thank dear Jim Brennan), moral support, endless transcribing, and linguistic accuracy

Katherine Tegen, for her ongoing faith and editorial guidance

Julie Hittman and Anya Belanger, for their willing assistance, efficiency, and enthusiasm

Steve Sauer, for continued encouragement and championship

And to our families for their patience and love

Other books you might enjoy in the Julie Andrews Collection:

BLUE WOLF by Catherine Creedon

DUMPY AND THE FIREFIGHTERS
by Julie Andrews Edwards and Emma Walton Hamilton,
illustrated by Tony Walton

DUMPY TO THE RESCUE!
by Julie Andrews Edwards and Emma Walton Hamilton,
illustrated by Tony Walton

DUMPY'S APPLE SHOP
by Julie Andrews Edwards and Emma Walton Hamilton,
illustrated by Tony Walton

GRATEFUL: A Song of Giving Thanks
by John Bucchino, illustrated by Anna-Liisa Hakkarainen

THE LAST OF THE REALLY GREAT WHANGDOODLES
by Julie Andrews Edwards

THE LEGEND OF HOLLY CLAUS by Brittney Ryan

THE LITTLE GREY MEN by BB
illustrated by Denys Watkins-Pitchford

MANDY by Julie Andrews Edwards

SIMEON'S GIFT
by Julie Andrews Edwards and Emma Walton Hamilton,
illustrated by Gennady Spirin

Also by Julie Andrews Edwards

Hc 0-06-021805-3
Pb 0-06-440314-9

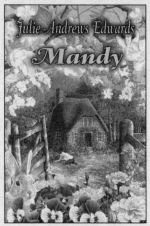

Pb 0-06-440296-7

The Last of the Really Great Whangdoodles

Ben, Tom, and Lindy Potter have never heard of a Whangdoodle until they meet Professor Savant. He tells them all about the wise and magical creature who disappeared to another land because people stopped believing in him. When the professor invites them on a quest to find the Whangdoodle, they can't resist.

Mandy

When ten-year-old Mandy discovers a tiny abandoned cottage in the forest, she is happy to finally find a place of her own. She is so determined to keep her new refuge a secret, she even lies about it. But what happens when Mandy becomes ill and no one knows where to find her?

■ HarperTrophy®
An Imprint of HarperCollinsPublishers

Words. Wisdom. Wonder.
www.julieandrewscollection.com

■ HarperCollins*Children'sBooks*
www.harperchildrens.com